The Wimp Dragon Tales

Bedtime Stories for Kids

80+ Inspirational Sleep Travels for Children for Overcome Insomnia, Build Confidence and Achieve Deep Sleep Quickly. [Dragons, Wizards, Unicorns...]

By

First Time Mum University

Download the Audio Book Version of This Book for FREE

If you love listening to audio books on-the-go, I have great news for you. You can download the audio book version of this book for FREE just by signing up for a FREE 30-day audible trial! See below for more details!

Audible Trial Benefits

As an audible customer, you will receive the below benefits with your 30-day free trial:

- FREE audible book copy of this book
- After the trial, you will get 1 credit each month to use on any audiobook
- Your credits automatically roll over to the next month if you don't use them
- Choose from Audible's 200,000 + titles
- Listen anywhere with the Audible app across multiple devices
- Make easy, no-hassle exchanges of any audiobook you don't love
- Keep your audiobooks forever, even if you cancel your membership
- And much more

Click the links below to get started!

For Audible US

For Audible UK

For Audible FR

For Audible DE

Table of Contents

Introduction

Tell me one story. How many times have they told you to do this? When you're a mom, mother, grandparent, uncle, aunt, babysitter, child-care worker, or someone else still has interaction with babies, I'm sure you haven't missed this regular plea for childhood. Yet have you ever asked what children want when they apply? Are they just looking for entertainment? Do they want to fly into a dream world? Would they like the connection between storyteller and listener of the intimate relationship that exists? Are they trying to connect with a character that can represent what they want to be? Are they looking for explanations of how they will act in practice, explain or cope?

Here there is a basic principle: Children love stories — for several purposes. If we need evidence, just listen to them say, "Please tell me a story." Look at the rows and rows of children's stories books which fill our bookstores and libraries. Look at the stories that come to life in popular children's movies, or the tales of strife, war, and triumph that appear to be the focus of too many video games. This is our appetite for stories we never stop wanting to hear them, even though the form of the questions can change somewhat—"Can I get a new book? "And" Can we borrow a DVD? "The focus of this book is on the pragmatics of sharing tales, discovering metaphor solutions, and structuring your own psychological myths, rather than reiterating the basic metaphor therapy studies. Since both the art and science of metaphor therapy are relevant, at the end of the novel, I have included a comprehensive reference section that will enable interested readers to further explore the essence of metaphors as a language medium, their usefulness study, and the variety of their therapeutic uses. It can also help you discover more educational story content in a range of ways, from children's books to traditional folktales to Web pages. This book has compiled stories for kids of all ages. From fables to inspirational an adventurous stories, all have been beautifully presented.

Chapter 1: Bedtime stories for kids – An Introduction

A bedtime story is a popular storytelling method, where a child is informed at bedtime to encourage the child for sleep. The bedtime story has long been regarded as "a definite entity in many families" Reading bedtime stories provides multiple benefits for both parents and children. A bedtime story's set sequence before sleeping will boost the growth of the child's brain, language comprehension, and critical thought skills. The connection between the storyteller and listener establishes an emotional link between the parent and the infant. Because of a child's "power of imitative impulse," the adult and the tales they say serve as a role model for the infant to obey. Bedtime stories are often valuable for showing the infant moral values such as compassion, selflessness, and self-control, since most children are known to be "naturally compassionate because they have encountered or can understand others' emotions" Therefore, bedtime stories may be used to explore deeper topics such since death and bigotry. As the bedtime stories grow in scope, the infant can "grow in their understanding of other people's lives and emotions"

1.1 History of Bedtime stories

Nap-time tale is a popular storytelling method, where a child is informed at nap-time to be encouraged for sleep. Nap-time stories provide many advantages, especially for family / elders and kids. A bedtime story's set ritual just before sleep has a calming impact, and an individual's soothing voice telling a tale makes it harder for the infant to fall asleep. The interpersonal dimension establishes a link among the narrator as well as the audience. Bedtime stories may could be narrated from a journal, or the storyteller may create them. The stories are generally not very long with happily climax. A common type of reading at bedtime utilizes longer books, but breaks them up, therefore they build plot twists. Kids look forward to tales in bedtime, so they will have a set schedule in place. There aren't real "beginnings" to how nap-time tales began as storytelling has been a piece of heritage of world in general as civilization began. The notion of contemporary bedtime tale arose out of traditional storytelling though. Family and fellows would labor hard throughout the day before the industrial revolution; the parents as well as the babies. People will sit round the bonfire at the sunset to chat and share tales of gossip. After the novel, all parents and kids will sleep in the evening together. The tales would include controversy, emotional pain or exploration which parents and children will hear to. With the rise of capitalism, at different hours and in different spaces, parents and children started to go to bed. Schedules were developed for Bedtime. Another main predictor was the transition from verbal story-telling to a book reading. Since the Digital Revolution, the publishers of books were intensely aggressive in seeking to market as much as possible of the finest material. Stories like in Peter Pan were beautiful, joyous and colored. The publishing firms started transitioning to the three-to-six year old age range after WW1. The tale had started to become quite easy. Today most reported bedtime stories with a rather mild vocabulary are from one-to-five min. long. The kids would know the tales the parents would tell in the past which were really bleak and gruesome. Brothers Grimm's were some of the best known legends. And as civilization expanded, the tales changed to make us lighter and happier. Bedtime stories appear to wind up with a sort of morale. Older bedtime books were very detailed and violent, so the lessons were often detailed and violent. A famous illustration is the Sandman, which would spray sand in children's eyes at night while they were sleeping. Bedtime tales will also incorporate other values for children while they're adults. Early on Disney was really well recognized along with Snow White & Sleeping Beauty to represent a pure woman who likes to sweep. Disney's page is distinct from the Brothers Grimm page.

1.2 Importance of bedtime stories

Children would often ready for sleep, climb into their beds and wait for their parents to read a book until they fall asleep. The classic stories of the fairytale, imaginative books with cartoon drawings and more were piled up high next to their bed waiting to be read every night.

Just like the narrator confronting a dilemma in these novels, bedtime stories face their own problem: they're dying. A recent study showed that a third of parents rarely read their kids a story at night and that 4 percent of kids don't own a single book. Furthermore, a survey in the UK in 2010 showed that 55.7 per cent of primary school teachers taught children who had never read a story.

As the stories about bedtime are diminishing, so are the benefits that the children get from them. It has been proven that reading to an infant before bedtime improves academic achievement. As reading is introduced into the daily life of a child, as they get older, they will have an internal motivation to read. Research has found that children who read for fun are more likely than those who rarely pick up a book to do better in math and English.

Reading is essential to helping children grow as writers. Pie Corbett, a literature specialist and former head teacher at the high school, said: Any teacher still thinks the greatest authors, the most professional authors, are learners. It not only provides the language to youngsters, it also builds their imaginations.

Most parents said lack of time and uncertainty prohibit them from reading to their children every night. Some also said that their kids prefer the books over TV, gadgets and computer games. Yet parents need to note that this time it's all about enjoying time together with their child and developing together.

Bedtime tales are not just for educational benefit. Much of the time, tales are beautifully constructed with a lesson on emotional existence which is subconsciously instilled. These teachings are applied to teenagers and adults including the following from some of my favorite childhood books:

Where the Wild Things Are Mauric Sendak: there are monsters all around us in the universe, yet you can take care of any circumstance in which you are, conquer the monsters and return to a safe location.

The Sharing Vine, Shel Silverstein: We are all growing old but together we grow strong. We will be appreciative of where we come from and when we end up.

For so many merits of Nap-time stories it is our responsibility to make time for our family. There are too many options to discover stories these days-bookstores have wide parts for youngsters, libraries are always free and filled of content, and e-books and online tales are now open to everyone due to technology.

So consider what you did during your childhood the next time your kid gets ready for bed (a study says 91 percent of parents read bedtime stories as an infant)). Choose a book from the bedside table, and read your child to sleep.

1.3 The secrets of ideal bedtime story

Many parents have combined the literature greats with Hollywood blockbusters trends to build bedtime tales to inform their youngsters. But the formula for the ultimate tale of bedtime has now been first revealed.

- **Bedtime phenomenon: scientist creates books that bring children that sleep in minutes:** Protagonists should involve the dragon, with magician & the sprite, said the families that took part in the poll, which would preferably revolve around a magical palace.

Children said they welcomed a fleeting moment of suspense in which the hero is confronted before eventually triumphing over the dark powers.

According to almost all those surveyed with most kids shunning love tales in favor of fiction a happy ending is important.

- Why incarcerated dads use bedtime stories to communicate with their children The study also showed that one in ten parents fear that their capacity to say stories is not up to scratch. About half of the children surveyed felt that when the storyteller used various vocals for every role player, tales were most amusing.

A fifth of teenagers said they were anticipating the plot to turn well for all.

Researchers consider August and September to be the most painful time of the year for parents to let their kids go off to sleep. Parents say during the summer break, they tried to bring the kids settled into a bedtime schedule. The lengthy summer season days often provided parents with a task.

Story-telling expert Alex Charalambous said: "When your baby plans to just go back into school since the holida ys are over, a consistent nap time plan including reading the story is a wonderful thought to set up. The simplicity of a traditional tale pulls children in, as the evidence indicates, and the positive outcome allows for a good night's sleep.

"The story box is perfect means of sharing a novel. Story boxes could be a box of shoe & painted as a background, woodland or a scene on the seaside. For your characters you might use finger marionette and roles who are trapped on lollysticks. This helps you to give the story a lot of room whatever direction you want. "Dermot King, Butlin's managing director who commissioned the research, addedWe have been working to account for the under-fives in each possible way, while ensuring that families may spend more time around the kids despite additional stress. "To insure that nap-time is an experience like the remaining part of the day, we're renting out these creative story boxes at the beach, offering parents the opportunity to truly involve their kids at nap-time, & make sure they're sleeping off in anticipation for another day-long action."

1.4 How to read a bedtime story

Research shows that when dads read the stories of bedtime, their children perform better at school. Bedtime stories promote the growth of expression and vocabulary, which make children appreciate acquiring reading skills. If nothing else, a snooze-time story aids in establishing healthy sleep habits. Then, time to tell some tall stories.

Get into the characters: Bedtime stories can be told in a comfortable environment-so let's continue by shutting off the television. And introduce some dramatization to the tales, whenever appropriate. Seek to interpret in various languages, or do any of the acts the protagonists of the novel do. Anything that makes this tale more interesting would make it more enjoyable story-time.

Have a daily read: If your child only learns to speak, read the same story on a regular basis. It would help them grow their vocabulary and strengthen their memory. The first time a kid listens to a tale they won't catch it all — but hearing it over and over again makes them get familiar with vocabulary and develop rhythms of expression.

Stop making the story-time into a learning activity by utilizing it to check the reading abilities of your infant. Instead, only ask specific questions about the stories and help them create a link with the tale and their everyday lives. For instance: "What will you do?" or "Any some other black cats?" Book a Boys' Night In it's much more necessary for fathers to consciously inspire their sons to learn. Boys still think of reading as a 'girly' activity to do — which might understand why lads fare too poorly in literacy testing — but once young boys see their primary role model loving reading, it would always inspire them. In reality, the Mr. Men stories don't always have to be that. Reeling off your favorite line or two from a newspaper article, novel, comic book, or football match day system can help them create a connection between reading and playing.

Find age level: At the library, spend some quality time with your family. Look for age-oriented novels, and stories you loved as a kid. Let those even select books— even if they want one that is too complicated for them but them like the images. Encourage them to look about to discover tales that they want. In school children who have favorite books seem to perform well when they are small.

1.5 The Merits of bed-time stories

Bed-time stories are considered to promote relationships between parents and children and to ready kids to asleep. Although researchers have lately added certain forces to this nocturnal activity. They claim that when you along with your kid sail to the place of the Wildness with Max or study green eggs and Sam, you are literally stimulating the growth of your kid's cognitive abilities.

"Neural evidence suggests that children grow a lot more than we ever considered feasible while parents and care takers communicate orally with them — this involves narrating to them," as said by G. Reid Lyon, director of the NICS and Human Development's infant growth and behavior division in Bethesda. Those improvements vary from enhanced reasoning abilities to reduced stress rates. But maybe the greatest advantage found recently is the scheme bed-time stories will rewire the minds of children to sharpen their language mastery.

"This is a strong evidence of a cognitive disparity between children those which are read daily, & children who haven't," says Dr. Lyon. The positive thing is that differences will not be lasting. Scientists have shown in NICHD research that visual photographs of children's brains deemed weak readers reveal no involvement in verbal-processing regions. Though subsequently the study spent 8 weeks recitation to the bad readers for one to two hours a day and working out certain learning activities, their mind function had shifted to resemble as of the successful students.

This is how the retraction happens: as you read to your kid the traditional bedtime tale of Margaret Wise Brown Goodnight Moon, exaggerate oo vocal in the moon and draw the locution hush, you activate associations in the portion of her mind which processes linguistic vocals (auditory cortex). There are forty four of such sounds in English, named phonemes, which vary from ee-ss. The more times an infant hears certain signals, the easier it learns to perceive it. After that when she is a baby learning to understand English, she'll be capable of discern the distinction between, perhaps, the words big and doll more quickly. As a school grader acquire to recite, on the screen, she would be more likely to sound foreign words out.

"You will first learn the parts to tear down unfamiliar terms into bits," Dr. Lyon says. "For example, when children hear the term cat, they typically listen it wrap up like one voice (cat) in lieu of 3 (c.a.t),"so he speaks. "But when told to tell cat less with c, they can more readily realize about words that are made of single vocal, thereby eliminating the cuh sound to render at." Reciting rhymes to children is a mean to develop this ability.

Creating an Inner Vocabulary Parents should use story-time as a starting stone for communication to improve the language abilities of a child even further, narrates Lise Eliot, Ph.d AP of neuroscience at Chicago Medical Facility & writer of what's going on in there? How the mind & brain grows during Life's starting 5 Years. For e.g., if a mother points to the baseball cap of Curious George and tells her boy, "Do you have a cap such like this?" she gives him practice in proper language use.

Dr. Eliot, though, warns parent not to constantly fix speech errors created by their infant. "My own kid still thinks he's, like 'That's the hat for him,'" she notes. "So I'm not thinking, 'No, you can tell his hat,' as you do not want to deter him. Instead, I'm only teaching the appropriate expression by accurately repeating his phrase: 'Yeah! It's his hat!'" Over time, communicating with a kid can broaden the language much further than only talking to her would. That's how books will expose children to concepts & things — like kangaroos or porridge — which are not part of their immediate world and often not piece of their everyday communication. Watch out for tales that include especially vivid or vibrant vocabulary, such as the working of Caldecott winner William Steig, He also drops into his books four-star terms like scatter brained and languid.

"One More Moment!" This statement is commonly considered as straightforward attempt by a kid to postpone bedtime. Yet what children & guardians may not realize is that regular reading of a book will assist a kid improve his or her reasoning capabilities.

The initial moment kids read a novel, they don't remember it all, narrates Virginia Walter, Ph.Ds. an assistant professor at the, Los Angeles' University of California. graduate school of education and communication sciences. However when they listen that over and over again, they tend to recognize trends and loops, knowing if single page asks, " bear brown, what you watch?" the forthcoming page would inform the answer of brown bear: "I watch a blue bird staring me." They will even start to anticipate what's going to occur next depending on their previous experience ("Ooo, the wolf wish to break down the house!"). Afterwards, such topics in pattern detection, series comprehension, and forecasting results will benefit kids in many fields, ranging science and math to music and literature. Reciting loudly does not have to end until children can read alone; in addition, that is where they improve literacy skills in reading, says Dr. Walter. To work, inquires a kid how she feels is going to happen after that, or whether she will finish a tale otherwise.

Experts say parents uphold the practice even in adolescence. You'll start to introduce her to latest terms and add and her repertoire by picking books that are just over a teen's ability level. Moreover, reading aloud will offer a forum for discussions with the children.

"Talking about difficult problem outside of the background of your daily existence is a much better," states Dr. Walter. "If the problem pops about even in private life, one might ask, 'Recall we spoke about what?'" She recommends reading Katherine's iconic Bridge towards Terabithia for talking to teens about death; similarly, the small Home on the Prairie books gives families the chance to address prejudice.

Soothing Snuggles: The interactions of an infant to books must be fun to help impart the educational advantages of literacy, narrates Peter Gorski, M.D "You desire him to conjugate reciting with fun and emotional warmth, above all else," he says.

The Moment children are relaxed and secure they will also lessen their anxiety levels by reading aloud. The moment a kid is undergoing some pressure — like being teased or beginning a new school — his brain tries to shield him by releasing the hormones cortisol that stimulates the body's reaction to "fight/flight." Cortisol may in turn help children withstand everyday tension in limited numbers. Although it may inhibit learning in greater numbers.

Although no experimental experiments have been done about how bedtime books impact children with elevated cortisol rates, neuro-scientists believe it is rational that reading a popular book when snuggling next to a parent will relax an infant, thus reducing the cortisol levels to help him focus better, Snuggle up in a cozy spot with your boy, with his favorite covers & animals stuffed alongside to enhance the calming nature of the story-time at your home.

"Calm down & enjoy your boy," says Dr Gorski. "Just imagine about the near time you're spent together can do with your cortisol rates

Global Institute of Infant Welfare & Human Growth Director of Child Development & Behavior Division Reid Lyon narrates: "Neural evidence indicates that when parents and caregivers communicate orally with infants — like narrating for them — children understand even better than we ever thought possible." For years to come, you can continue the essential type of stimulation. MomJunction asks you where you can start reading your kid's books, what sort of stories you can hear, story-telling rewards and a few infant bedtime tales. Introduction of the infant into the realm of tales is never too early. Doctors suggest you start reading them from a very early age for baby stories to boost her imagination. In fact, while you are still pregnant you can make a habit of reading aloud, as babies recognize the voice of their mother in the womb.

It is a good habit to set aside time to read the stories every day. The perfect hours are bedtime, and naptime. Getting your baby read a portion of the night time routine will help settle down and realize that it's time to sleep. Set time between 6.30pm and

8.30pm, anywhere. Might cause your little one exhausted every time after that.

Bedtime stories are a perfect way to boost your kid and you connect. She'll love to look at the colorful pictures and listen to the fairy tales in real good time. Numerous other advantages (1) are listed here:

1. Develops comprehension: Story reading helps build oral speech skills, listening skills, memory and language processing skills for your infant. It is a safe opportunity from a very early age to strengthen her language and multiple sentence structures.

Over maturity and age your kid can learn to interact in the same manner as you by body language, communication techniques, listening and learning.

By the time they reach one (2), babies will have learned all the sounds needed to talk their native language. The more you learn, the more phrases the less becomes revealed.

2. Social and emotional development: drawings and stories go hand in hand, so your kid will come up with ideas regarding assorted objects, plants, birds, etc. You'll hear her using new words for thought, experiencing and sharing her emotions.

3. Cognitive abilities: Long before your baby starts speaking, she absorbs information about the language by listening to the stories that you are reading. This will certainly reap benefits as your child starts their schooling.

Babies can learn to turn pages around for about ten months and listen to new sounds. As your little one continues to grow she'd learn from left to right the art of reading. Through listening to bedtime stories, children, who are around a year old, will improve their problem-solving skills.

4. Improves attention: Involving your baby in bedtime stories is a perfect way to help her grow acquainted with the practice of reading. It's a very good and safe habit too. By reading to her every night, you will develop their concentration skills.

5. Relieves anxiety: Calming her mind and body is a safe way to go to bed. Particularly though she is over-stimulated, the reading of stories will help her get interested in a whole new environment and release her from all the anxieties.

6. Improves personality and knowledge: As your baby ages, she may start searching for and taking inspiration from other people. Reading time is the best moment to affect the little kid, and to show them lessons about life. Which can enhance her personality and expertise.

7. Is a ritual: It becomes a practice and part of her life when you make story-reading the norm of your little one. Gradually reading is a treat, and when she grows up you don't have to remind her to learn it. The reading can open the door to writing later in life.

1.6. Tips for Parents

- You must not make your baby and yourself hearing stories monotonous. Keep it so fascinating that she looks forward every day to this type of relationship with you.
- Using various feelings and vocal noises when reading the tale helps the kid to learn socially and emotionally.
- Let your baby look and answer questions while you listen, in order to encourage emotional learning and thought skills.
- Let her imitate noises, recognize pictures and study vocabulary.
- Print it out of exhilaration, excitement and closeness. It allows them to connect themselves with children.
- While reading, cuddling helps your baby feel connected, protected and wet.
- Sing rhymes, and make amusing noises like wildlife.
- Don't think about hearing the same tale over and over again. Love babies, and learn from repetition.
- Switch off triggers such as Cable, or radio.
- You will strengthen associations in the portion of your baby's brain that understands language sounds by exaggerating the 'oo' sound in the sky, and utilizing phrases like hush. The portion is known as the auditory cortex.

- Know the contact with your kid is the secret to getting the best of the story-reading on bed-time.

1.7 Stories that you should read to your kids

Any easy narrative with fun drawings should fit for children. They'll affect your baby's overall growth. For children, choose basic short stories relevant to their present stage of existence, such as how a boy found his missing pet or how a girl discovered how to use the potty seat.

Stories with the right images will show assorted dolls, creatures, birds and more to your little one. Stories with minor information like the variation in color, form and scale will allow her to differentiate between the choices available. But try them out.

Young babies cannot recognise the images, but because their vision is still improving, they get drawn to various shapes and contrasting colours. Add stories with a message in it, and your kid can understand certain values for the lessons of her lifetime.

1. Good Night, Gorilla by Peggy Rathmann: There was a zoo full of species such as lion, wolf, bear, horse, mouse, cat, rhino and more. The zookeeper makes nocturnal runs at night and heads back to his house. The zookeeper completed his rounds that day, and was making his way home. A mischievous gorilla then snatched his keys and went after him. It liberated all the other animals one after the other from their cages. The zookeeper was pursued and they went into his room. The keeper's wife got the mean creatures found. She will lead them back to their rooms. All the animals returned to their homes.

2. Margaret Wise Brown's Escaped Rabbit, illustrated by Clement Hurd: There had been a young rabbit there. She felt depressed one day, and tried to run away from her mother and become a wall. The mother was more afraid as she cherished to the heart the little rabbit. She promised the little one she would accompany her anywhere she was heading. The Mother's unconditional affection made the young bunny feel healthy and happy. She went to bed happily, holding her beloved mother!!

3. Good Night, Patsy Scarry's Little Bear; illustrated by Richard Scarry: Once there was a little bear that loved his dad too much! Both also appreciated the company of each other. Since the father came home they played together every hour. The father bear recounted to the little one a tale of bedtime during supper. The father will hold the little one on his back after the bedtime tale, and send him to bed. The baby bear had concealed someplace one day. The father went on to playfully hunt for the infant, asking, "Where might Little Bear be? "The father looked high and low-above the china cabinet, outside in the woodbox, under the stove to locate him. Father had not been able to locate the little child. Finally, as they went by a mirror the little bear showed itself. The little bear walks to bed (believing he had fooled his father).

4. A Sung Na Book of Sleep: As the night is dim and the moon shines brilliantly, everybody goes to sleep. Except a vigilant owl!

One owl was up on a starry night observing all the other creatures settling down for the night. It has seen some animals standing up sleeping and some lying on the move! She had some nights there, happily. Some become dead entirely. Every animal has its own resting spot!

5. Margaret Wise Brown and Clement Hurd Goodnight Moon: There was a tiny rabbit who often acted kindly and talked respectfully. Everybody around had enjoyed it. The bunny says "goodnight" to all around "goodnight room" every night, before going to bed. Healthy evening Sky. The cow running over the moon Goodnight. Goodnight, and the gold balloon...' The little rabbit, like the sky, the comb, the broom, the bowl of mush and the cow jumping over the roof, says goodnight to the rhyming items in his house. And lastly, go to work.

6. Guess How Much I Love You by Sam McBratney and Anita Jeram: A little bunny is adorable and always likes his mum! One day he decided to show just how amazing his affection for his mother is. The parent bunny and the little bunny are exchanging comments of growing affectionate language. As the match comes to a end, all relax into night.

7. Llama, Llama, Red Pajama, by Anna Dewdney: This is a bedtime for Baby Llama. Yet the little guy isn't yet able to go to bed with his mother. He asks where she's gone, and likes to think until she comes back. Momma reassures that she is "still near, even though she is not here now." This calming tone allows the little one to slip into a peaceful sleep.

8. Rest At Last by Jill Murphy: It's late in the night, so they both find their way to bed tiredly. You are now able to fall asleep. But why do Mr. Bear not fall asleep? It's because the baby bear is still busy with planes. And mommy bear is snoring now .. Snoring! Mr Bear asks if he really gets some quiet!

9. Nick Sharratt Timothy Pope's Shark: In the Park continues staring through his mirror, now and again. He stared through the telescope into the water, and saw a shark in the bay. But how could it happen? Sure, the finding might only be the fur of a cat or uncle!

10. Julia Donaldson's Monkey Puzzle: Once split a little monkey from his mother. He loved his mum, and tried to locate her. He'd asked a butterfly for support. Support him the nice butterfly decided. Yet butterfly didn't realize if it felt like the mum monkey. Through when the butterfly attempted to suit the mother of the monkey it struggled. During through mismatch the butterfly's silliness made us laugh.

For babies a bedtime tale brings them to an imaginative place, where fun never seems to stop. Telling tales and conversing with babies can be treated as seriously as feeding them. Allow bedtime story- telling your kid one of the best moments. Only don't hesitate making it into a routine!

Chapter 2: Bedtime Fables for Kids

A fable is an imaginary story and is intended to convey a moral lesson. In a fable, protagonists are typically animals whose words and actions represent human conduct. A type of folk literature, one of the progymnasmata is the fable too. Some of the best known fables are those credited to Aesop, a sixth-century BC woman who resided in Greece.

Variance on the Fabrication of the Fox & the Grapes: ""A hungry fox noticed several spikes of plum dark grape dangling off a trellised tree. She attempted using all the tactics to reach at them, yet she wearied out in vain, because she couldn't not touch them. Eventually, she walked away, covering her frustration then saying: 'the grapes are rotten, but not plum as I thought.' "MORAL: Do not revile anything outside your control." MORAL: Do not revile anything beyond your reach."

"'Alas,' the fox said, displaying a super conscious smile, 'I've learned about it previously. In 12th century, a regular fox of normal nature should have expended his time and power in the futile effort to hit distant ferment grapes. However, praise to my familiarization of vine growing, I've found at once that much tallness & width of the creeper, the flow on the sap by the increased amount of varicose vegetables; 'this is fox's old story, and the grapes. Have you ever seen the Fox story and the berries, sir? One day, the fox was. "Oh, indeed,' Murphy said, who, as fond of nonsense like he had been, couldn't bear fox & the grapes for the fresh." They're nasty,' the fox said.

"'Yes,' Murphy said, 'the story of the capital.' "Oh, the fables are so good!" Wiggins said.

"Everything the rubbish!'The contradictor stated diminutive. 'Drivel, all drivel; ludicrous material of speaking aves & beasts! As though someone should accept these things.' "I do—-for single one,' Murphy stated.' (Lover Samuel, Convenient Andy: A Story of Irish Living, 1907)

2.1. The Bear That Set Alone

"There once lived a brown bear in the forests in West that could handle it or leave it go. He might visit to a bar there they palm off mead, a sweet drink made in honey, and only have 2 drinks. So he would bring some money into the bar and tell, 'Look bears will get what,' then he would go home. Ultimately he was a prominent teetotaler and an influential instructor on temperance. He'd warn anyone that arrived at his home about the horrible consequences of alcohol and he'd joke how healthy and good he'd been after he forgo skimming the things. To show that, he will balance on head & hands and spin the house's cartwheels, push down the umbrella frame, turn off the lights of bridge, & smash his elbows on walls. Instead, exhausted from his balanced workout, he will get laid on the concrete, and move for bed. His better half was in great pain, and his kids were in great terror.

"Moral: you could just as easily collapse flat on your face and lean backwards too much."

2.2. The cock and the pearl

Once upon a time, a crow was strutting up and down among the hens in the farmyard, until he unexpectedly spied something sparkling among the straw. "Oh! Hey, yeah! 'Quoth, 'that's for me,' and it quickly sprung from under the grass. What turned out to be just a Gem that had been misplaced in the yard at any chance? 'You may be a joy to people who value you,' quotes Master Egg, 'but I would rather have a single barley-corn for me than a peck of pearls.' Precious objects are for all who can value them.

2.3. The wolf and the lamb

For quite some period a Wolf sat lapping on a mountain at a spring while, gazing around, what would he see anyway a Lamb barely starting to sip back a little bit. 'There's my dinner,' he said, 'if just I could seek an reason to take it.' He instead yelled to the Lamb, 'How could you muddle the waters I drinks from? 'No, no, no,' said Lambkin; 'if the water is dirty up there, I can't be the source of it, because it's flowing over through you to me.' 'Well then,' said the Wolf, 'why would you label me terrible titles each year? 'That can't be,' said the Lamb; 'I'm just 6 months old.' 'I don't know,' snapped the Wolf; 'if it wasn't you, it was your father;' so for this he rushed over the weak little Lamb and.'' Yet she has screamed since she died. "Any excuse would be representing a tyrant."

2.4. The dog & his shadow

It happens a Dog caught a slice of meat & took it to his house in its mouth to enjoy it in comfort. Then on his way home, he have to pass a frontier lying over a flowing marsh. He glanced down as he walked, and found his own reflection reflecting on the water below. Assuming it was a special dog with a particular slice of beef, he decided to get one too. And he took a glance on the water at the eye, but when he turned his mouth open the slice of meat slipped out, fell in the sea & was not sighted again.

Beware lest by grabbing the shadow the meat will be lost by you.

2.5. The Lion's share

The Lion, along with the Duck, the Jackal, and the Wolf once went a-hunt. They hunted and hunted until they caught a Stag at last, and they then lost their lives. Next came the issue of whether to break up the waste.

'Quarter me this Stag,' the Lion roared; so it was skinned by the other creatures, and split into four sections. Then the Lion stood before the carcass and imposed judgment: the first quarter is for me in my capacity as King of Beasts; the second quarter is mine as an arbiter; another quarter falls to me in the chase for my part; and as for the fourth quarter, well, as for that, I would like to see which of you will try to put a hand on it.' 'Humph,' the Fox grumbled as he walked away.

2.6. The Wolf and the crane

An animal he had slaughtered had been gorged by a wolf until unexpectedly a little bone in the meat caught in his mouth, and he did not chew it. Soon he experienced intense pressure in his chest, and jumped up and down, groaning and trying something to relieve the discomfort. He was trying to persuade everyone that he encountered to cut the tooth. 'I'd give something,' he replied, 'if you'd let it out.' The Crane eventually decided to offer, and asked the Wolf to lay on his side and spread his jaws as wide as he could. Then the Crane placed its long neck down the throat of the Bear, and loosened the bone with its beak, before it actually pulled it out. 'Were you gracious enough to give me the incentive you promised? 'Crane said. The Wolf smiled and revealed his teeth, saying: 'Be happy. You put your head into the jaws of a Fox, then comfortably pulled it out again; this would be enough praise for you.' Respect then envy should not go together.

2.7. The man & the snake

Through chance, a Compatriot's son came across the mouth of a Serpent, which twisted and stabbed him to death. The father in anger had his pole, then chopped off half of his tail by chasing the Serpent. Then the vengeance snake began stinging some of the cattle's of Farmer and causing serious damage to him. Ok, the farmer felt it better to patch with snake, and took honey & food to his lair's head, and asked him: 'Let's forgive & forget; possibly you were correct to threaten my kid & take vengeance on my livestock, but I was correct to want and vengeance him; currently that we're both happy, why shouldn't we can be friends? 'Nope,' replied the snake; 'spare your presents; you cannot overlook the demise of your friend, neither I the loss of my tail.'

2.8. The City Mouse and the Village Mouse

You have to learn that once in a while a Town rodent goes on a country trip at his uncle's place. He was not sophisticated, this uncle, though he liked his friend in the town and he accepted him heartily. What he had to sell were beans and eggs, cheese and potatoes, but he gave them safe. At this country fare, the Town rodent really turned his lengthy nose up & stated: 'I don't imagine, Cousin, In which way you get going with such bad food like this, though certainly you can't imagine good in the world; come & I will help you learn how to eat. A week when you are in town, you're going to ask how you've ever been able to tolerate a country existence.' the 2 mice left & returned mid night at the city Mouse home. 'When the long journey ends, you'll like some refreshment,' the friendly Town Mouse said, and brought his friend to a very big dining hall. They noticed the remnants of a delicious Food at that place and immediately the 2 mice started eating cakes and jellies & all the stuff which was sweet. All of a sudden they heard howling & barking. 'Country mouse' said. 'What is it? 'It's only the house dogs,' the other responded. 'Ah! 'Country mouse' said. 'On my dinner I don't love this music.' At that instance the door opened, two big watch dogs came in, & the 2 mice had to scam and run off. 'Well done, Cousin,' the country rodent said, 'What! Soon? Soon? 'And the other told.

'Indeed,' he replied; 'More, pleasant beans & bacon despite cookies, and fear wine.

2.9. The crow & the Fox

A Fox one day saw a Crow was flying away in his beak with a cheese's piece and settle down on a tree branch. 'For me it's like I'm a Fox,' Master Reynard said, and he started walking up to the tree's foot. 'Good morning, Lady Crow,' he said.

'How good you feel today: how vivid your feathers are; how luminous your eye is feel confident to have your tone will overshadow that of most birds, even as your appearance is doing; allow me hearing only one melody of you, so I can welcome you as the Goddess of Birds. "The Crow turned her head or tried to catch the finest, however the instant she opened her mouth, the cheese fragment collapsed to the ground, just to be captured by Master Fox. 'That's going to do,' he said. 'I just needed that. I will send you a bit of wisdom about the time to come in return for your milk. 'Do not like flatterers.'

2.10. The giddy Lion

A Lion was reach the end of its life, so laid sick and tired in his cave's window, struggling to breathe. The animals gathered alongside him & inched closer as he grew increasingly vulnerable. They said to themselves before they saw him on edge of death: "Now's the time to claim off old rivalries." Therefore the Badger came then aimed its horns toward him; after that a Bull booted him by his antlers; and the Lion lay powerless before them: so the

Donkey, knowing very protected of risk, stepped up and turned his butt to the Lion, kicked his feet in his head. "This is a twofold burial," the Lion muttered. Insult the fading glory just through cowards.

2.11. The Ass and the Lapdog

One day, a Farmer came to the stables to see his burden beasts: his favorite Ass was among them, who was often well treated and always carrying his owner. His Lapdog, who jumped and licked his face and frisked just as pleased as possible, came with the Farmer. The Farmer felt in his pocket, gave some dainty food to the Lapdog, and sat down while he gave his orders to his servants. The Lapdog hopped into the lap of his owner, and laid dreaming there while the Farmer rubbed his paws. Seeing that, the Ass broke free from his halter and started to imitate the Lapdog. The Farmer was unable to keep his hands from laughter, so the Butt went up to him and tried to crawl onto his lap by placing his paws on the Farmer's back. The Farmer's servants charged with sticks and pitchforks and quickly told the Ass that no comment is sloppy jesting.

2.12. The Miller Mouse & Jack the Lion

Once a Lion rested, a very little Rat started running up and down over him; this quickly stoked up that Lion, who put his huge hand on the rat and extended his wide jaws to consume him. "God forgive, O Lord," the little Rodent pleaded, "chastise me this chance, I'll not overlook it: who cares, but I might be capable of helping you any of these days?" The Lion was really startled at the Worm's suggestion that he should make him raise his hand but let him go. The week after the Lion was trapped in a net, and thus the attackers whom wished to take him to the Emperor safe chained him to a tree as they took the place of the cart to take him on. Only then the little rodent walked through, and she saw the terrible state the Lion is in, she goes up with him and quickly nibbled through the ropes that tied the King of the Animals. "Wasn't I correct?" Mickey asked. "Little buddies can appear to be better partners and a sympathy can go a fair way."

2.13. The Swallow and the Other Birds

This occurred in a field where a Swallow and several other birds were hopping around picking up their food a Countryman was seeding several hemp seeds. 'Watch out for that man,' the Swallow quotes. 'Why is he doing what? 'And the others told. 'That's hemp seed he's sowing; be sure to pick up one of the pods, or else you'll apologize.' The birds paid little attention to the words of the Swallow, so by so large the hemp grew up and was formed into ropes, so all of the birds who had hated the guidance of the Swallow were trapped in nets formed of that same hemp. 'What am I asking you? 'Swallow said. Doom the seed of evil or it will flourish to your doom.

2.14. The frogs desiring a king

The Frogs existed as happily as they could in a marshy area that was only right for them; they splashed around worrying for no one and no one was bothering them. Yet some of them felt that was unfair, they were meant to have a king and a good constitution, and they agreed to submit Jove a petition to give them what they needed. 'Mighty Jove,' they yelled, 'give us a king who will reign over us and hold us in control.' Jove chuckled at their croaking, and dropped a massive Log down into the marsh, which sprung down to the swamp.

The Frogs were terrified of the commotion in their midst from their nests, and all fled to the bank to look at the hideous monster; but after a moment, seeing that it did not rise, one or two of the boldest of them went out toward the Log, and even tried to approach it; but it did not move. Then the biggest hero of the Frogs leapt onto the Log and started to dance up and down on it, and so all the Frogs came and did the same thing; so for a while the Frogs went on their business every day without having the slightest note of their new King Log lying between them. But that didn't match them, so they sent Jove another petition and said to him, 'We want a real king; one who will truly rule over us.' So this made Jove furious, so he sent a huge Stork among them, who soon set to work to consume them all. The Frogs then repented, because it was too late.

No regulation is better than cruel regulation.

2.15. The Mountains in Labour

One day the countrymen found that the mountains were in labour; smoke poured from their summits, the ground quaked at their feet, trees were falling and large rocks were tumbling. They felt confident something terrible might happen. They all gathered in one location to see what a horrible idea this could be. They were hoping and waiting but nothing was arriving. Then there was a much more powerful earthquake, and a large crack in the side of the mountains emerged. They both dropped to their knees, hoping. Inevitably, and finally, a teeny, tiny mouse peaked out of the distance her little head and bristles and came rushing down towards them, and ever since they had said: 'Much uproar, no consequence.'

2.16. The Hares and the frogs

The Hares were being hunted so often by the other beasts that they did not know where to go. They had backed off as soon as they heard a single object chasing them. One day they noticed a group of wild horses stamping about, and in such a panic all the hares were scuttling hard at a stream, ready to kill themselves rather than exist in such a perpetual state of terror. But just as they got close to the lake's shore, a troop of Frogs frightened off in effect by the Hares' arrival, and jumped into the sea. 'Truly,' one of the Hares said, 'things aren't as horrible as they seem to be: 'There is still somebody worse off than you.'

2.17. The wolf and the kid

A Kid was perched on top of a building, and a Wolf walked beneath him looking down. He suddenly started reviling his opponent and assaulting him. 'Murderer and rapist,' he screamed, 'why are you here in the houses of decent folks? How dare you make an appearance where they learn your filthy deeds? 'Curse back, my young mate,' the Wolf said.

'Being brave from a safe distance' is simple.

2.18. The woodman and the serpent

A Woodman was trampling home from his job one wintry day when he spotted something lying black on the ground.

As he got near he realized that everything but dead was a Hydra. But as he ran home he picked it up and put it in his bosom to warm up. He set the Serpent down on the hearth before the flames as soon as he got indoors. The kids watched it, and eventually saw it coming back to life. Then one of them stooped to pet her back, but the Serpent lifted his head and stuck out his fangs and was about to bite the girl to death. And the Woodman grabbed his arm, and sliced the Serpent in two in one stroke.

'Ah,' he said, 'No indebtedness from the evil.'

2.19. The bald man and the fly

Once upon a time there was a Bald Guy who stood up on a sunny summer day after work. A Fly came up and kept circling around his bald pate, and sometimes stinging him. The Man was looking for a hit to his little rival, but axe palm then fell on his head; the Fly again tormented him, but this time the Man was smarter and said: 'You can only hurt yourself if you find disgusting friends.'

2.20. The fox and the stork

The Fox and the Stork had been on friendly terms at one point and appeared to be really close friends. So the Fox welcomed the Stork to have dinner, and placed nothing in a rather shallow dish before her for a joke except some broth. It the Fox might quickly suck up, but the Stork might only wet in it the end of her long cap, and leave the meal as hungry as she ended. 'Sorry,' the Fox said, 'the broth is not of your taste.' 'Pray not of apologize,' the Stork added. 'I hope you'll come back to this stay and dine with me early.' So a day was scheduled for the Fox to meet the Stork; but when they sat at the table, all they had for their dinner was stored in a very long-necked container with a small mouth through which the Fox couldn't put his snout, and all he could do was lick the exterior of the bottle.

'I'm not going to apologize for dinner,' the Stork said: 'One terrible turn needs another terrible turn.'

2.21. The fox and the mask

A Fox had fallen into a theatre's store-room through certain way. Then he noticed a man looming over him and began to be really scared; then looking closely he realized it was just a mask that performers used to place on their head. 'Ah,' the Fox said, 'you look really fine; it's a shame you've got no brains.' Outside exhibit is a bad match for inner merit.

2.22. The jay and the peacock

A Jay venturing through a yard where Peacocks used to play, discovered a collection of feathers that had come out of the Peacocks when they molted. He bound both of them to his legs, strutting down among the peacocks. They quickly noticed the thief as he came near them, and striding toward him pecked at him and plucked his stolen plumes down. And the Jay couldn't do anything than head back to the other Jays, who had seen his actions from a distance; but they were almost as irritated with him, stating to him: 'Not just good feathers make great birds.'

2.23. The fox and the ox

'Oh Dad,' a little Frog said to the big one sitting next to a pond, 'I've seen such a awful creature! It was as high as a mountain, with horns on its head and a long neck, and it had hoofs split into two.' 'Tush, boy, tush,' the old Frog said, 'that was just the Ox of Farmer White. It's not that wide either; maybe he's a little taller than I am, but I could easily render myself as broad; you just see.' So he blew himself out, blew himself out, and blew himself out. 'Was he taller than that? 'And he inquired.

'Oh, so much bigger than that,' the young Frog said.

The old man blew himself out again, and told the young man if the Ox was as large as that.

The response was: 'Better, dad, bigger.'

So the Frog took a deep breath and breathed and pumped, and swelled and swelled. And then he said: 'I'm sure the Ox isn't as heavy as He's bursting at this point.

The boastful and excessively self-regarding attitude will contribute to self-destruction.

2.24. Androcles

Once a slave called Androcles betrayed his owner and ran into the jungle. When he walked around, he stumbled across a sleeping Cat, crying and grumbling. Firstly he started to run, but realizing that he was not chased by the Lion, he turned around & moved towards him. As he approached, the lion took out his foot, which was all bruised and wounded, and Androcles noticed an enormous prick in it caused all the suffering. He took the spike out and tied the lion's foot, which was quickly able to get up and kiss Androcles' hand like a puppy. The lion therefore brought Androcles to his den, and used to carry him meal each day to survive from. Although after short period of time both the Androcles & the Lion were caught, and the detainee was condemned to be hurled at the Lion, Lion had been held for many days without food. The Emperor was present to witness the event, along with all his party, & Androcles had been lead into the center of the field. Soon the Lion was freed from his lair, and charged toward his prey, roaring and bounding. But as soon as he got close to Androcles, he remembered his buddy and fawned at him, kissing his paws like a happy puppy. Amazed at this, the Emperor called Androcles, who asked him the entire thing. Afterwards the detainee was forgiven and released, and the Lion was freed to go into his native forest.

Great fullness is the expression of virtuous hearts.

2.25. The Bat, the Birds and the Beasts

A great fight between the Birds and the Beasts just about to break off. The Bat debated whom to pursue once the 2 groups were gathered around. The Birds who crossed his ledge retorted: "Come with all of us;" though he said: "I am indeed a Beast." Then, several Beasts that crossed below him googled and said: "Join with us;" though he said: "I am still a Bird." Fortunately, during the last minute there has been calm, as there was no war, so the Bat returned to the Birds so wanted to join in the delights, yet they all twisted toward him and he had to take flight. He therefore returned to the Beasts, but they decided to bid an escape soon, or else they'd tear him to bits. "Oh," the Bat stated, "I get it now," He who is neither one nor the other has no mates.

2.26. The hart and the hunter

The Hart once drunk from a stream, so enjoyed the solid character he had crafted therein. 'Oh,' he said, 'where you sees these glorious horns, a cervid like that! I wish I could carry quite a beautiful crown with somewhat appropriate legs; it's a disappointment they're too slim or thin.' At the instant an Archer stepped across and fired a whistling arrow at him.

Far sped the Hart, and quickly he became nearly out of reach of the Attacker with the strength of his speedy limbs; but not knowing where he had been heading, he went under some bushes with roots rising low whereby his horns became entangled, so the Attacker had time to deal.

'Sorrow to me! Forgive me, apologies! 'The Hart shouted: 'We still dislike offer to us whatever is of higher importance.'

2.27. The serpent and the file

A Snake walked into an armourer's store in the midst of its wanderings. As he glided over the floor he noticed a file lying there pricked his face. He twisted on it in fury and attempted to stab his fangs into it; but he couldn't do much damage to heavy iron, so he had to give up his anger early.

There is no point in targeting the ignorant.

2.28. The man and the wood

One day a man came into a forest with an axis in his side, asking all the trees to give him a little branch he needed for a special reason. The Trees were kind-natured and offered him one branch of their own. How the Man did, then put it in the head of the pole, and then got to work chopping tree after tree. The Trees then saw how stupid they had been in supplying their opponent with the ability to kill themselves.

2.29. The wolf and the dog

A gaunt Wolf was almost dead from starvation when he encountered a passing House-dog. 'Ah, Uncle,' the Dog answered. 'I understand how it could be; you'll soon have your distracted life ruined. How do not you work like I am doing, and have your food supplied to you regularly? 'I wouldn't protest,' said the Wolf, 'if I could just get a spot.' 'I'll quickly organize it for you,' said the Dog; 'come to my owner with me and you'll share my job.' So the Wolf and the Dog went to the city together. The Wolf found on the way there that the fur on some portion of the Dog's choker was falling down very badly, and he asked him if it had happened.

'Ah, this is nothing,' the Dog said. 'That's just the place the choker is put on at night to keep me chained; it gaffes a little, but one gets familiar very soon.' That's it? 'The Wolf said. 'So, Master Dog, farewell to you.' Starving free is better than being fat captives.

2.30. The belly and the members

This occurred to the leaders of the body one fine day when they were doing all the job and the Belly was eating all the meals and snacks. So they had a conference, and after a long debate, they voted to strike work before the Belly wanted to take their fair share of the job. And the Hands declined to eat the food for a day or two, the Mouth refused to consider it, and the Teeth did not have much job to do. But after a day or two, the participants began to realize that they were not in a really good state themselves: the hands could barely function, and the mouth was all parched and swollen, whilst the legs could not bear the rest. And they realized that only the Belly was performing the required work for the Body in its boring, silent manner, and that it needed to work together or the Body was going to fall to bits.

Chapter 3: Bedtime Fables to help with learning

Fable is, commonly speaking, much more true than reality, since fable portrays a man as he was in his own day, the truth presents him as he is several centuries later to a group of inconsamerable antiquarians. Fable is more historical than reality, as truth informs us about one individual and fable informs us about one million people. "Of all the various forms of counselling, I believe the best, and what pleases the most uniformly, is fable, in whatever type it exists. Whether we find this method of teaching or therapy, it excels all the others, as it is the least surprising and the least arbitrary. For the purposes of the narrative, we peruse the speaker and interpret the precepts rather than his guidance as our own assumptions. Morals imperceptibly insinuate themselves, we are trained by accident, and are oblivious, smarter and stronger. In short, a man is so much over-reached by this approach that he feels he is leading himself as he follows another's orders, and therefore he is not receptive to what is the most awkward situation of guidance.

3.1. Tweety the bird

Once upon a time there was a name for bird Tweety. She really likes messaging. And she's kind of very sweet. And she really likes music. She was the youngest baby bird. But she has been really sweet. She cherished her parents much like she had cherished herself.

She likes to listen to the songs and she wants to perform it.

It was a first day at school for Tweety. Next to her, she stared at the chickens, which were big and smaller. She kept singing each time she was in college. The other birds began teasing her after a while claiming she's nuts and tiny and she'll never be a artist.

She fled to her house from college, and went to her place. She raced for the mountains where she could see the stars. It was her dream place she'd visit every day.

Tweety is dwelling on the stuff they thought about her. She looked sadly at the heavens. Throughout her view, Tweety felt that I don't know what they're doing about me, it just matters what I think of myself. Using a telescope, Tweety gazed at the planets, then exclaimed. She noted that the planets are all the shades of the spectrum as you gaze through a telescope. Yet they were just light, without the telescope. Then, Tweety composed a poem about planets.

It was she who was inspired. So, she began blogging. Tweety asked her mother to send her to a singing festival for a couple days. We stayed in the vehicle and drove home. It was time for the meeting. Tweety went first! Tweety became irritated. Yet Tweety was no longer tense, though. She'd started to record. The magistrates then declared the winners. And it was Tweety who played!

Tweety was the most popular performer, after years and years. Both the songs of Tweety became popular, and the story's philosophy was named "Tweety the Star"

Moral: "Follow your dreams."

3.2. <u>Geire, the Wolf who tried to flee</u>

"I'm venturing north to live a new future." They were the final phrases his soldier learned from Alpha Zolon. We had lived to difficult periods, so had plenty of soldier Geire. Knowing the danger of becoming a lone man, he chose to leave his clan at the right moment. When he said farewell, much of the group grumbled at him, realizing that the arrogant wolf had abandoned them to quietly willow away. But Zolon politely bid Geire goodbye, and left him to last a week or two with prey. Geire was glad and he took off. Which takes us into the present.

Geire had already begun to regret abandoning his old clan. Another clan who discovered him hidden in the forest not far from their camp had almost killed him, hoping to capture some of their food. He took a mouse, and snarled it down. A group of scouts, however, scented dead mouse but their hunting patrol has not yet been sent out. They had suspected that it was an attacker. To run from their furious clutches, Geire had to scamper up a steep mountain slope. He was watching now, missed their efforts to leap and strike him with their jaws. He barely survived. Geire returned happily to his old home, and discovered that no matter what struggle he had to go through, he had at least members of his home to support him get through. It took them a while to have him recognized again, but he was content in the end.

3.3. Gigantic or super smart

Once upon a time there was a Giant who was so tall that he could see through the tallest mountain of the world.

One day the Giant meets a girl that is really tiny. No, not as tiny as Tom Thumb in the fairy tale but she is not too much taller.

"Hello, Mister Giant," says the girl when she sees the Giant: "gosh, you are big, guy!" Hello, little child,"says the Giant: "that is because you are so tiny." The Giant and the little child burst out laughter.

"Say, Big, what can you do what I cannot do?" asks the girl.

"I can move really fast," replies the Giant.

"But, not as quickly as I can," says the kid.

"Oh, no, I must teach you," says the Giant as he plans to take an immense measure of one mile.

Since she is so small, the Giant does not realize that she catches the lace of his boots. Right before he sets down his foot, the girl let go the lace and lands right in front of the Giant.

"What took you so long?" questions the girl to the Giant, who cannot believe his eyes that she is standing in front of him.

"Are you the same kid as before or are you her twin sister?" He's stammering.

"I don't have a mom," the girl says, "but I have a brother who's much smaller than I am because he's just raised." The giant laughs loudly: "He's not as little as you are, but he's a little bitsy boy." "You're sure you can do anything better than me?" The kid questions.

"Of course, little sweetheart, I can see out there the big peak." "Well, go ahead and tell me what you've seen," the girl responds.

"I'm going to put on my cap first, because the light is bright in my hair," the Giant says.

The kid poses next to a large cap for the Giants. She easily places herself at the bottom of the hat right before he lifts it up and place it on its top.

She will gaze up beyond the mountains on top of the Giants shoulders. Much ahead she will see a white lighthouse at the blue bay. A red painted ship with brown sails lies down on the water.

She feels the huge sigh, and she grips the edge tightly as she sees his large hand move for his cap. Luckily the Giant kindly lays his cap down on a plate. He doesn't notice how the girl was sliding down a chair leg.

"Do you go where?" Asks the giant who sees the girl there.

"I'm here, Mister Giant," the girl says: "I'm going to tell you three things you've seen around the range." Laughing embarrasses the Giant's chest. He asks: "Alright, little smart thing, tell me." "There was a very blue sea first of all," says the girl The Giants eyes wide open.

"There was a big white lighthouse second" he now lifts his eye brows.

"Fourth, there was a lovely red-colored ship on the water." Unexpectedly, the Giants mouth falls open.

"Can't do it. That is a bruise, "he babbles.

"Dear my darling Giant, did you note the unusual color of the ship's sails? They were not white as normal but dark. "The Giant did not believe his ears.

"How can this be, it's impossible," he desperately says.

The girl mocks: "Should I offer up something, nice Giant?" Ah, yes, just let me learn how this operates," the Giant begs.

"Oh, Giant love," the girl smiles: "Smart has to be the one who isn't tall!"

3.4. Daisy pumpkin's elephant shadow

A little girl named Daisy Pumpkin woke a dawn with face of a completely developed African Elephant because of a mix up by a very excellently known but rather incompetent shadow seamstress. Daisy stood before a wide wall and waited disbelievingly as the shadow of the elephant mirrored every step. As she raised her back, the face of the elephant shifted her ears, moving from same by same with her tail. As Daisy jumped on one knee to get the reflection made so. She leapt, skip, twirled and repeated her precisely every moment she did the shadow of the elephant. That wasn't what any extent of the possibility expected of Daisy. Eventually, a couple of people arrived to witness why the small belle was running and spinning outsame the building. The instance they witnessed Daisy's elephant shadow the people were surprised.

'That is wonderful,' an old elderly woman.

'That's superb,' an elderly guy said. 'That's witchcraft,' a very old lady said.

A crowd had in very less period and they were all hustling and rushing to get up to the frontend to see Daisy and the sight of her elephant. Daisy was just an average little girl up to that point but she was somewhat different now. Public requested her for signatures and requested that she take pictures for them.

'Run on it,' a tiny boy yelled.

'Go a turn,' another said.

'Hold on your hands,' a small belle yelled.

Daisy followed what they requested of her & she felt dizzy after some time, what to do with obeying the wishes of everyone. That was the peculiars experience. She went to sleep the night before as a normal little girl and was the focus of attention now. She was unable to go outsame anywhere from that day on, without public starring & pointing. Within 24 hours Daisy turned from a simple regular little belle to a celebrity and a superstar. The local press stated her a Gift for Good. It was named a scientific phenomenon by a magazine. Customers have been demanding photos and autographs wherever she goes. People got anxious to see the shadow of the elephant, and would shout at Daisy to make it spin, jump, and twirl. She passed the summer vacations with superstar actors and pop stars attending parties, and premieres. She gave interview to famous magazines, television shows and was a guest for tea with the Queen. Daisy was happiest than anyone who ever claimed he was happy.

Suddenly on a day, at the recess of the summer, Daisy danced at park as a grumbling black cloud drifted across the region and halted facing the light. The park was gone dark, and Daisy's elephant shadow was gone as swiftly as it was surfaced. The crowd hissed & chanted for the image of the elephant to return. Daisy entreated them to sit. She started to dance but in absence of the threat of the elephant copying her steps Daisy was simply an ordinary little belle who loved to perform. The audience got annoyed and started leaving the park letting Daisy to play alone and no one to. It began to rain and to thunder. Daisy squelched home dowsed with sloshy shoes and a streaked face with tears and without any glimpse of the shadow of her elephant. A few weeks passed and the appearance of the elephant just became a vision. It was dark, and gloomy every day. Puddles lined pavements, and abandoned ornaments were park benches. No one called for any more photos, and nobody gave her invitation to premieres and parties. Living was so dreary as to deter Daisy from moving out. Day after day she remained at house in her pyjamas, looking out of her bedroom window, praying and hoping for the sun to rise once more.

3.5. Unity is strength

The Sticks There were two boys called Tom and Robert in a kingdom Once. Live on a cow. The Elder brother was Robert. They will fight forever. If they buy something for Tom from their aunt, Robert would get mad and battle and vice versa.

One day their father had agreed to have a contest. A bundle of sticks was up there. "The one that splits the stick package gets a candy bar" their father said. The former was Robert. He did his hardest but had not been able to crack it. Next was Tom. He did his hardest but still he couldn't. Their father ordered that the boys smash the bunch of sticks. They answered "Giving it a shot is worth it." The boys were stunned. The set was literally split. They were very pleased and each got a chocolate bar. They made apologies one to the other. They recognized that cohesion was power. They agreed they should never fight again, just remain there and support one another. After that they lived together.

3.6. Turtle and rabbit story

A neanderthal named Ug the Thug existed there some five thousands, four hundred and sixty-six years ago. He resamed overlooking a desolate canyon, but was desolate even then anywhere. He used to have a top club and fuzzy shoes and he loved chasing after stuff and most of all scaring them. Ug the Thug had been mean to all he knew. If the stuff he faced was large or small, it didn't really matter if he wanted to give it a shake. He loved to play as hard so he could.

"Raaaar! 'Aaargh!' 'And and' Graah! 'His dream sounds were some of his. In the evening, Ug the Thug retired to his hole. He stood alongsame his blazing fire, eating as much food so he could. He drew images of himself on grotto and even he felt very content with himself.

But no-one really liked Ug the Criminal. All were terrified of him, so remained as far away from it as possible from him. No-one ever headed to, or even moved past, his cavern. They have held to them. And one evening he spotted a falling star when Ug the Thug stood by the bed in the cellar. There was a great white illumination flowing through the skies and he was gasping. It was magnificent. Ug the Thug looked at the skies and he thought he had a mate for first point in his life, so that he could ask them all of what he had witnessed. Ug the Thug felt sad for the first stage in his career. He stepped out the next day in his shoes he would not roar and clatter along. He then came down to the river flowing via the high grass and stood there, painfully staring at his reflections in the water. It happens that even a rodent that had crossed the river higher dropped into the waters at that very instant then started to squeeze and flap its hands in the air so it couldn't swim. Ug the Thug sat down to take a look at the rodent. Without thought, he put out an arm that was as large as a brick and very carefully raised the rodent onto the bank of the river.

However, anything occurred next day. Ug the Thug had only just woke up as he noticed small feet pattering-patter. Everyone walked in. This was the rodent. And thus the rat was holding a rose in its hands. The rodent throw down the rose at Ug's foot then stared up towards him with its wide brown eyes.

The Thug dropped sameways into Ug. He fell beyond his cavern in the desert, utterly shocked. He knew that the rose was a mouse kudos-you. He'd just found a partner! He felt so glad he started singing. He gets up and danced joyfully about the grotto. He felt amazing he was wading over the water, humming again. To all he knew he could not resist grinning. Folks became afraid initially. Is it even conceivable that Ug the Thug will be comfortable and affable? Isn't he just loud and aggressive? However in the ending they started believing that to be real, smiling back and holding palms with Ug and laughing with laughter too.

After a while that no one was anymore scared of him. He left asame his poor lonely house, and came to stay with all the others. He made many friends, and then never felt alone. And he was eventually named Ug the Hug, as this was really what he wanted to do most.

3.7. The Warrior

There was once a guerrilla there. Okay he's been bold for stong and everything just not as widely recognized as he'd expected. And he went down a street one day, and encountered a black smith. He thought of his strengths and his worries. The black Smith told him that we too are one of a kind of his talents. For he was not only able to render the finest weapons on earth but it was also sorcery.

Unfortunately the warrior wasn't very big, but the blacksmith said he didn't care about being willing to compensate him "little by little" in due time. And they partnered up and went on the most exciting and glorious journey across the world, becoming the country's wealthiest and most successful hero. That his enchantment armour rendered him invincible.

So until he had enough of funds he asked the blacksmith again let me pay you. Right now I'm the wealthiest guy in the land ...... the blacksmith said why you've got sir little by little with every spell I've put on your shield that took your existence day. Your mortgage is paid off, and then you will die.

Offer, lend & Take

3.8. Mommy

There resamed a Monarch in a glorious fortress on the sea coast. In pregnancy the poor bloke had lost his wife even because she had given life to the first daughter, Duchess Selena. The King did never let his tiny girl, Selena, from under view after that terrible day, because he realized he wouldn't be capable of living to himself if something occurred to her, also.

One afternoon, Princess Selena told her father: "Papa, couldn't you put my arm if later today we go to the seafront?"For all this, dear girl, you're very little." "Oh, Father, just for a while! "You could slip and injure yourself." "No, Dad, if you're holding my arm, the children do not want to interact with me." "I advised you, sweet darling, now you are too little." The Ruler hugged his baby farewell fell asleep. But, Royal Selena had been so depressed that she wasted practically the whole night weeping.

"If I could interact with the children for a bit ..." plagued her feelings.

The girl woke ill the day after, and was unable to get off of bed the whole day. Its status remained constant one day after. And a whole week elapsed. Poor Selena's cough wouldn't crack with the finest medics in the realm taking better care of them. At about the same period the two deities, Violet and pinky, began doing hide-and-seek between the clouds of paradise.

"Run, it's your time," Pinky screamed.

"I no longer intend to play," Violet responded.

"What, then? "Since playing for only the 2 of us is tedious." "Not so! "Replied Pinky, annoyed.

"And so, it is! "At that point God's word reverberated:" Shouldn't battle, girls." "Kindly, Lord, please send us a buddy to have joy of, "Violet begged with zeal.

"Purple, understand me. Two are only a handful but three are far too many! "God's word replied.

"But only the 2 of us are lonely," Violet persistently kept on.

"There is always error with all that," screamed Pinky.

"I'm just no longer talking to anyone! "Bitten by his argument, Violet interjected.

"As though it was I who cared! "Pinky wept, upset much more, until he sailed south.

"Violet, two are very few yet three are enough," echoed God's sound.

"Blablabla-blah-blah ...." teased Violet.

"Well maybe. And let it be! "The word of Christ reflected through the heavens. The sickness almost instantly overwhelmed Royal Selena back on earth, and she turned her head feebly.

The unfortunate King was not able to get over her fragile body in his embrace.

"rise up, Selena," he called out. Yet the fairy didn't raise her face, because she was still playing with Pinky in the clouds at the time.

Eventually, the dream of the young girl had come to pass, and she did not have enough of the fun and mutual laughter with her best pet, Pinky.

"Pinky, in just a short period you clearly forgot so much about me," Violet proclaimed with frustration the next day.

"You didn't tell me you didn't play alongsame me? When I was too dull. What, still, is tedious? "As he proceeded to interact with Little Selena, Pinky's conceited answer arrived.

Violet has said nothing. She is about to shift away of everyone, until she overhead God's speech.

"Won't you inquire to get a buddy playing? What else are you screaming, right today? "And I've lost my mate." "If you don't listen to me, that's what happens." "I need Pinky back," the angel began crying more.

"Alright, Violet, I'm making your fantasy come true, but unless you convince me whatever the motivation of it all is." "Two are so few, but 3 are too many." "Yes! "So the word of God answered. But by then, Beauty Selena in her dad's arms raised her face.

Gladly the King whisked, but his grin quickly wavered.

"Papa, I was having a blast in the sky. We were doing anything we liked. So you weren't anywhere, so I needed you. ".." "It is all my responsibility," howled the King. "You fell ill because of me, my kid. I just about lost everything ... My dear girl, I am never going to discourage you from doing whatever. I'll tell you! "When we're at the pool, you won't take me by the same? ""This is right. I'm not going to." "Thank you very much, Father, "marveled the princess.

Everybody was free, finally.

At a shore, Royal Selena made several new mates, whereas the 2 angels, Pinky & Violet, became together than ever before.

And the years went by.

Future queen Selena grew even more, till the the moment she wed Prince Kodor, the courageous and lovely.

But while they lived in peace and joy, for a number of years their cradle stayed barren of a descendent.

It wasn't much until the empire's people began to fear there was no successor to the crown, although Prince Kodor & Princess Selena were ill of despair.

This was then that Violet drifted around clouds to clouds in paradise, searching of Pinky.

"Ha, you're back. I was searching for you." "Why did you ask me? "Pinky questioned.

"What would you say, how do you think? 'Playing, of course.' "Violet, I no longer want to play." "Pinky, why do you not want to play? "And I've been playing with Princess Selena for so long. She was so kind and sweet. I just want her! "And the word of God rang across the skies: 'Want to meet her again? "Yeah, indeed! "Pinky shouted happily.

"Alright, I'm going to give you over to her, so you're going to call her 'Mommy.' Would you agree? "Yes. Yet what's 'Mum?' '"You're going to have to find out," God's word replied, as Violet began crying.

"Pinky, what will I do without you? "Who said you're going to be without him? Hehe-ha-ha ... "The 2 angels discovered themselves in the heart of Princess Selena, as long as God began to chuckle. 09 months after the King traveled to see her when the girl finally gave life.

"Dear girl, you're going to always be twice as careful now as you're taking good care of your spouse & your first child."

"What is so humorous about that? "The King inquired. "Move with me into the nursery and you can see for yourself," he was told by Mistress Selena.

Upon reaching the crib, the King have not see one but two crèches.

"Do you now see why I smiled, Papa? This is that I have 2 sons. The duchess happily declared that this is Pinky in the pink cradle, and Violet — in the purple same.

First the King was dumbstruck with gladness. Yet shortly afterwards, he returned with himself and began to worry about his child once more.

"Dear child, two kids offer joy double but still double the obligations." "Avoid thinking about me so much, Papa. I am an adult and a Mama! "The Finish

3.9. The Rabbit's foot and Anna

Anna was called to her senses by a sudden rap at the door and she rushed and watched that who was outsame.

'Hi Anna, where's the Mommy? 'The milkman Mick told, laughing.

'She's been out,' Anna replied, taking the liter of milk gently and setting it onto the kitchen counter, not trying to pay him for it.

Mick frowned at his hairy chin and rubbed it. He patted Anna's thick blond platinum hair, 'Well, I will see her other time, take care smile.' 'Take care, Mick.' Anna absently shuttled the gate and started watching out of the balcony, but despite watching what was going on outsame, she easily slipped into her fantasy universe of fairies and elves dreaming. She leapt as she noticed the opening of the back entrance, and her mum turned up packed with grocery bags and looked cranky.

'Have you paid Mick a milk peddling for that? 'I missed' whoops! "What? I advised you there was some cash in the cupboard. Anna, you're a cynic but you never listen. At minimum, you'd feel I would depend on you. Now you are the only kid in the house so you're 8, not 4! I had enough of it, Anna! If just your dad were always present, but not just at college, he hardly took much obligation for you girls,' she concluded lamely.

Immediately, Anna felt very confused, her mum was constantly reminding her, & just her children. They can get off with something, just for being girls.

'I have just forgotten, mother. It's never my mistake.' Then whose mistake it is consamer that to be? Many times you are being much too sneaky to please me! 'Anna had a withering rub across her thighs with that.

Wise with discomfort, Anna felt that this cannot be a wise thing absent from here for a bit, so she went back upstairs to sleep under the pillow in the guest bedroom. She had something shoved up besame the rear wall in the gritty darkness. This was a small stitching box for mom. Anna stretched out, and raised the top cautiously. There were many jumbled knobs of all shapes and sizes hidden within, combined with pins, black yarn, scissors, tape, a rubber dandelion used for darting socks and some old fading sashes.

She took a bunch of bright buttons then started arranging these for groups of three, layups or occasionally even more. It was the foot of a little bunny on a necklace which caught her attention. o'I recall this, Grandfather brought that to fight but said it helped him secure in the war.' Anna's mom once told her this was a fortunate bunny's foot, but she felt it was funny as Anna stared at this one. He loved seeing the paws of rabbits onto bunnies while they were live, and not deceased! She punched on the rabbit's foot, rubbing it among her fingertips, the soft silky white hair. Erm ... She probably wouldn't, so how could her mother understand if she might just pulled out a bit of the rabbit foot? She will demonstrate it in front of Thumper, who is the grumpy old rabbit of her good friend Jimmy. She realized Jimmy cared nothing for him, and never washed out his cell. Anna has always think it tastes like smoke. She easily shut the stitching box, then slipped back down from below the bed on her bottom. Firmly gripping the foot of the bunny, she pranced down stairs, cautious not to fall on the edge of the wiggly floor. She was able to hear her mom in the dining room, sniffing the sour aroma of boiled brinjal. Nice, at good she was having a rough meal preparing but wouldn't hear her because she went by like a mist.

Anna raced down the paved lane, past the kids rolling the pavement with marbles.

'Hey, sweetie! 'Mr. Fielde, the aged gentlemen at numbered 57, motioned her around and Anna realized he tried to display to her Timmy's budie. Anna's mother told her that he had been a sad old man since the passing of his wife. He loved chatting to people, so his day was livened up. Anna and her dazzling blue eyes particular chatterbox. Anna accompanied the old man into his sitting room, where the door beyond them was locked. His portable Bakelite was spinning 'Broadway's Lullaby' and Anna decided to join along but she was not aware about the whole phrases.

'If you keep out the hand straight, I'll lie down Timmy and you'll be able to caress his belly.' Anna piped and easily put the foot of the rabbit into her purse. In her hands palms Timmy felt odd, so small, but moist and gentle. And as her tiny chest rise and went down, she could feel his heart pounding hard. His dark eyes flew this direction and that when he was startled by Anna. Rather scared than anything, he started chirping and Mr Fielde smiled.

'My feeling is that he enjoys you Anna.' Timmy jumped at the chance to float across the space and instead settled on the forehead of Anna.

'Ooooh! He's got sharpend claws.' 'It's OK, I'm going to lock him in cell, and Jack's just coming.' Jack was a fatty, over-fed ginger cat with a pink nose and a long tail stripes that was rubbing up to Anna's limbs whenever she came to see. She punched it, and he cooed to demonstrate that he was satisfied. Yet she realized that he did not like Timmy, as he just stood by his cages and watched him eat.

'Do you wish seeing my mystery?

What would that be? "See!' 'Anna displayed him the feet of the bunny.

'My God, The owner's name? 'My mother, she claims it's remarkable as it's the whole story she's left to know about my grandparents. He got it in the fight.' 'Do you realize how they are doing regarding the feet of a rabbit? You hold it into your pocket, and if you brush it, it will give you favorable luck, or also anything you've always longed for.' 'And it safeguarded my grandfather in the battle, so it should be nice! I will display it to Jimmy also, so I can't stay.' As Anna reached Jimmy's home, she was exhausted running so fast. She approached the door of Jimmy, and noticed it unlocked. Anna, at the back yard, would find anyone. It's not exactly a garden, just a barren concrete field with a damaged laundry line, an empty bathroom, a coal pit and several plants. Anna went straight to her mom's nursery where Jimmy was spanking out some shoes. Anna, in his enclosure, can see Thumper the bunny. He appeared upset. When his cover was windy white and now it was a muddy brown hue. His eyes had a dark and runny look. As he stuck through the torn metal sheeting, his nose quivered, searching for food.

'I've managed to display for you stuff,' she informed Thumper, bending down before his cell. 'At least you've got all the feet in it! 'She reached into her suit bag, looking for the foot of the bunny but removed her arm in terror. 'O goodness, there isn't one! 'What isn't it? 'So Jimmy called to come in.

'The foot of my dead rabbit' Anna stated regretfully.

'At first, you've never seen one,' Jimmy said, brushing her nostrils on her shirt.

'I might have missed it somehow, of course I did. I've got to find that because then I'm going to be in a major mess, I've only one hit today. I'm going to search for it.' On her journey back, Anna recalled that she was in Mr Fielde's room. 'May I left it in the living-room? 'Then she noticed that Mr Fielde had went out after pounding many times. She stood wretchedly on the road, back, uncertain how to do it. She crawled indoors after a moment, and was shocked seeing her mom leaned against the refrigerator, hands clasped, looking shrunken.

'Oh, where were you? "I had gone to visit alongsame Jimmy.' Anna glanced down at the dinner table and found her four siblings seated.

Getting the entire family together would be uncommon; normally some of them were absent. She found the stitching case, as well. Her heart sunk, particularly as her mom said, 'The foot of your Granddad's bunny has been lost, do anyone of you remember wherever it is? He also pledged lucky, particularly if a bullet skipped off his headset which would have destroyed grandpa in the battle. Given that Granddad's gone, I wear that as a sign of positive luck." 'No,' they all chorted, even Anna, who looked like she was going purple. The eyes of Anna's mom darkened eerily but she kept quiet and took the dinner away. In her mom's face, Anna saw the tragic expression and felt incredibly bad. She will certainly find it later, but also she lost her foot from the bunny where? What if somebody else snapped it up, so they'd keep it?

The next day, while she was going for the class, Anna passed a handful of ladies in a close circle. She saw ring chief Rosy. Rosy was the favorite of the educator who can do nothing wrong, but she still copied positive marks from other students.

'It's mine, I did notice it! 'Rosy kept, waving anything in air with pride.

'Did you notice what? 'Anna stated, as she leaned in to see what she had in her pocket, heart pounding.

'Just mine, my! 'Anna faded away as she saw the foot of her mother's bunny.

'The old cat which belonged to Mr Fielde played with it. Yeah, strikers of finds, nicks of failures! 'Hardly any!' 'The voice of Anna sounded clearly and loudly. 'It's my mom's, I'd give it to Jimmy, yesterday I had to leave it in Mr. Fielde's room. Send it in again! '6

'Shan, don't force me.' Anna consamered for a moment, 'If you don't let me get it, I'm going to put my bigger sibling on you then he's going to kick your face in.' Rosy smirked, 'Wow, do you suppose I care? No. No. I need a nickel for candy for the rabbit's foot.' The children's circle pressed in on Anna shouting, ' 'Anna realized it had not been a good statement. Rosy was a mischievous girl. She gave a slight turn, chewing her lips. 'Ok, I'm going to get the cash after dinner.' 'Ok, then after lunch. I'm going to be standing at the street for your lousy rabbit's foot.' As Anna's mother was talking to the woman nearest door, Anna went through the kitchen and snatched a quarter of the milk cash box. She felt bad, but she realized it was her opportunity to get back the foot of the bunny & make her mother content afterwards. She closely grabbed the penny and dashed into the corner to greet Rosy.

'Here's the quarter,' screamed Anna.

Rosy pulled it down and chuckled. 'My mom said that this was not the foot of a fortunate rabbit. Yesterday she smashed her first tea cup & my sibling knocked over the fire and lacerated his knee. It's not something we want in our home! 'It's fortunate you're a fake. My Grandfather was spared from becoming killed in battle! 'Anna hit Rosy with all of that, caught the foot of the bunny and ran back south. She could not even stop but realize that the foot of the bunny looked muddy and not pristine white any more. Her mum was going to be too mad.

7 Anna noticed her mom quarreling against her dad later that afternoon. 'A cent of the biscuit box has disappeared. You actually took it for you to go into the hotel bar! 'Anna's father's she yelled. Anna stood in the middle on one knee and put the foot of the bunny under her back immediately as her mother turned over towards her. 'I lose a cent, are you certain Anna didn't take it? 'She stared at him sad, her lips turned off.

'No,' another falsehood, to attach the one from overnight. 'How don't you ever accuse my siblings for this? It is me all the time, it is not reasonable! 'Anna ran straight upwards, she can see her mother cooking, preparing to explode, like luke warm water. She paused to hit the top, and heard.

'Since the foot of the bunny vanished, something went wrong here.' Her mother said her father angrily.

What will Anna do? The first reaction was to do away with it. She will cover the foot of the bunny under the lace curtains in the room of her parents, on the window ledge. This was theirs turn to bear the responsibility. It also just seems to Anna, however, they were able to keep playing in the building and not support. How Anna at that point hoped she might be a child! This will be forgotten quickly like for the cash.

Anna assumed without long that her mother would discover the foot of the rabbit, but that didn't really happen. Anna felt extremely bad every time the idea of a rabbit's foot kept coming up. Very rarely, Anna had seen the light eyes of her mom full of tears when she struggled to find them out where they it could be. 8 'None to know about now, Granddad. After all, not the fortunate rabbit's foot, it was? 'Sorry, her mother used to say.

Just like with Anna, by far the ugly portion, each time she got him at Jimmy's home, she stared at poor Thumper's feet, always buying a feeling of shame to her face.

3.10.   St. Uny Fairy school

There was once a fairy school named St Uny High and the fairies in that school were all exceptionally sweet. There was a very unique community of friends in the classroom, their names were Silvermist who wear a beautiful blue dress and the youngest of them all at the age of 14. And there was Idressa who was twelve and wearing a light sunburst coat. Next was 11-year-old Tinkerbell who wore an emerald green dress. Rosetta then arrived at the age of 10, wearing a ruby red coat. She was second at the age of nine and liked wearing her beautiful purple dress and eventually there was Fawn who was the smallest of all the girls at the age of eight who had an orange ginger jacket.

They played in the woods one weekend and an idea popped into Fawns head. "Oh, you men! Should we be going to Unicorn Meadow? "The friends were not so confident and quite scared but unwillingly decided. So they all went off to the meadow but the Unicorns had mysteriously disappeared before they entered the meadow, but luckily Silver mist could sense where they had gone through her special powers. She said, "Guys, they've gone over the hill to the meadow's Cold Same." Now the Cold Same was an area at Unicorn Meadow's furthest point, and its head teacher, Miss Lopez, strictly forbid any fairies to come near it. But the Unicorns were easily to be seen.

And the confidence was plucked up and they went up and over the slope. Not too far down they found one of the Unicorns, Vidia used the magic dust of her fairy to gather him up and bring him off on the safe hand. Tinkerbell then noticed another Unicorn and gathered it up with her fairy wand and sent him out on his journey. Next Idressa picked up a Horse, then Silver mist, then Fawn, then Rosetta, but only only one more. On they moved more and more to the Freezing Same before they encountered another pal who was the 15-year-old sister of Tinkerbelle, Periwinkle, who was wearing a snowy white dress and standing next to the last remaining Unicorn. Tinkerbelle replied, "Hello Sis," "why are you here? "Last night I had a weird vision," Periwinkle said, "I thought that the Unicorns were in danger so here I am, let's get this one gathered up and off to the safe same of the meadow." So Periwinkle swept her wand over her head to throw her magic on the Unicorn but ... something unusual occurred.

The clouds darkened, and the wind whispered as the leaves blew away from the trees. The thunder rumbled when a lightning bolt reached the earth just twenty yards from them. Suddenly their Head Trainer, Miss Lopez, appeared before them in the shape of a horrific old troll. Her complexion had a hideous green hue on her lips, and gross rough warts. Her hair was messy and knotty and her dress was nothing but rotting, dusty rags.

"Boys!" Miss Lopez exclaimed," I am angry with you all because I disobey my rules and come to the Cold Same of the meadow! "We didn't mean to come to the Cold Same of the meadow, but we had to get the Unicorns back to their field," Fawn asked, "What happened to you, Miss Lopez? "Miss Lopez said," It's who I am. It is here that I stay. I told you not to come to this location, but you did! And now that's where you're going to have to stay forever since you can't ever return home. Can't really come out of my secret really! "Suddenly in Miss Lopez's hand appeared a thick, bent, magic stick, raising it high above her head to cast her evil spell on the fairies, when Tinkerbelle suddenly screamed," Stop!!! You don't have to do that Miss Lopez. "Idressa added," You can come back with us and still be our Head Teacher.

"There's no need to live out here, Miss." Vidia stressed.

"You can still be a troll and a teacher in the head." Rossetta said, "But be a nice troll and a good teacher in the head."

Once again Miss Lopez's face screwed in anger as she raised her magic staff to cast her evil spell and all the fairies shouted "We love you, please come back with us! "After all," Tinkerbelle said, "we're all special, but we can all be respectful and compassionate." Miss Lopez's scowling face steadily softened as she progressively lowered her employees. Tears began streaming down her cheeks and a huge beaming grin emerged on her lips.

"Thank you for my lovely fairies," Miss Lopez said in a quieter voice now.

In the silver glow, Head teacher emerged from behind the fairies and wrapped like a dazzling twinkling robe around her. A second later the silver light disappeared and there before them sat a stunning young Miss Lopez. The fairies were posing with their mouths open.

Miss Lopez clarified, "You've just broken a 400-year-old curse that a wicked old sorceress put over me. The spell was to transform me into a Troll after the home time bell rang at the end of the school day which then put me back to life the next morning right before school began. I stayed here on the meadow's Cold Same and I couldn't fear all of you, my precious fairies. The spell can only be broken if either of my fairies, while I was in my Troll state, showed me goodness and affection and you did, I'm so thankful to you, my loves. "And with that, Miss Lopez gathered the last remaining Unicorn and turned to her lovely Fairies and said," Shall we go home ladies? "All of them grinned and embraced as they left to head to St Uny Big, where they all stayed happily afterwards!

3.11.   The snow mouse

Ears Rodent got up with a shiver, 'Brrrrrrrrrrrrrr' he muttered to himself, 'I'm in my comfortable room and my huge quilt but I'm always cold, my nose particularly.' The nose was nearly as fiery as the head of Ferdinand The Red Nose Reindeer. He placed his night cap over his head to keep his ears dry, and that he had placed many warm clothes over top over his duvet cover, because he figured it would be chilly that evening. He glanced at his watch on his nightstand, which said 8:45 a.m. – but he could n't really see any light coming via his windows as it would usually do at the early mornings.

Ears Mouse numbered one two and three then leapt out of bunk, rushing on to his wardrobe, taking his robe and pulling it in as fast as he should have. Then he moved on to his balcony and the shades raised. What he'd get was white things via his windshield, like very dense fog. He wanted to ignite his flame stronger so his room would be a little hotter. Through the use of an old sock and maybe some stalks, Ears Mouse attempted to have a fire started but a large drop of water will fall down the chute and put out the flames any time a strong fire traveled up to the ceiling. Ears Mouse felt he had to go there to explore. So he went equipped very rapidly, putting on his hottest jacket, his wellies, his gloves and his scarf. He raised his main gate and stepped through mist – or at best he was trying to do so. Ears Mouse jumped back to his house then fell to the floor on his middle. It hit him then-it wasn't rain, this was ice. He remembered that really transpired last night, 'it should 've snowed really significantly and blocked my chimney, gate and walls,' he said to himself.

So Ears Mouse became really concerned, 'how do I get out of here? 'He asked,' because I was preparing to pick a little more food for lunch, I don't have any stuff left throughout my pantry. He figured he had best start digging itself off just in scenario the ice won't melt for a couple of days, so he took his sled out of the kitchen drawer and lodged it in the ice at his doorstep. 'Hold on,' he said, 'where I position the ice I pull out.' He knew he was going to need to place it in his room. Ears Mouse had ice all over him for a little while, and looked like he was stuck in a cellar. He had always begun to feel really cold.

Stuff just looked a bit better outsame. That day, Jerry Jermie had already been searching for some sweet, nutritious caterpillars and sounded the alarm when he saw what has done to Ears Mouse's home. The ice had drifted down the lane throughout the night, as well as the strong wind made a cloud of ice around the property of Ears Mouse. Several of Ears Mouse's buddies are dreaming about what they can do to support get him into his freezing rain-covered home. There was so much ice to move the livestock using only aces and pickaxes. 'To make it look better, we should ask Bernie Pony to stomp on the ice,' Jerry Jermie stated. 'No, it could be too bad,' Sam Squirrel said, 'Heads Mouse might dug his path out to get stepped on.' "I get a notion," Lucy Mole said, "via the ice I might try to make a door." 'Did you ever burrow under snow before, Lucy? 'Dezzie Frog inquired. 'No,' Lucy replied, 'but it's supposed to be the same just a little colder. 'I think this is a brilliant idea,' Sam Squirrel said, 'is everybody in agreement? '. All decided that until now this was the right idea.

Lucy organized itself for her snow-walk. Sam Squirrel lent her his beanie hat that she was carrying on her nose to aid keep it dry. Jerry Jermie lent her his jumper despite the fact that it was made of gaps through his pointy beaks.

Lucy began digging via the freezing ice so fortunately it wasn't that difficult. In the meantime it was really chilly now down in Ears Mouse's house as Ears Mouse began looking a little dark. He hadn't tried to get through snow too much until the trigger of his sled snapped. Then he used his hands to reach via the ice and it was so chilly he couldn't reach his fingertips. Looking away from the ice and taking a break, Ears Mouse began to see stuff too. He could see a red dot in the air, and it became larger and larger. This was the red knit beanie that was sticking via the ice on Lucy Mole's nose then shortly afterwards Ears Mouse saw Lucy's eyes. 'I'm happy seeing you Lucy? 'I was really just about to freeze because I had to sit here for more,' Ears Mouse stated. He took a hug from Lucy and instead led Lucy back through the door.

When Lucy Mole & Ears Mouse each came out of the snow pipe there had been a large round of cheering. All mates of Ears Mouse have gathered over and given him a hug and a kiss. Sam Squirrel placed a nice warm cover over the shoulder of Ears Mouse and Jerry Jermie offered him a glass of hot water, becoming careful not to leave a gap in it from its points. They all returned to the location of Jerry Jermie, because he had lit a great fire.

Ears Mouse stood by the stove enjoying a delicious cup of vegetable broth, and quickly felt much colder.

The home of Jerry Jermie had been so cozy that other pets wanted to get out and create a snowman – a snowy mouse likes the buddy Ears Mouse.

3.12.   The Picnic (Ears mouse)

On the edge of a very small country village in England there is an old road called Pollies Lane. This lane leads to a small but beautiful forest called Oak View, which is not visited very often by people. All along this lane, if you were to look very carefully, you would find lots of holes – some big, some small and some very small. All of these holes are homes to various creatures – some big, some small and some very small. If you were to look even more closely you might see that just insame these holes there are doors – just like those on your house. And if you were very lucky to see into the holes, when the doors were opened of course, you might be very surprised to see that insame they are very like houses, just like the ones that you and I live in.One of the smallest houses in Pollies Lane belonged to a field mouse who's name was Ears Mouse. Ears Mouse was a very ordinary mouse except for one thing. . . . he had rather large ears for a mouse. All mice have very good hearing, but Ears Mouse's hearing was so good that he could hear a pin drop a mile away even with the door shut. Ears Mouse lived in a hole at the bottom of a very large, beautifully shaped, old oak tree. He built his house with the help of his many friends, most of whom lived in the lane or the nearby forest. It had taken about a week to build the house and then about another week to make all of the furniture. The front door was made from a few hazel twigs which were tied together with string. The windows were made from some broken glass that Ears Mouse found in the laneway near an old broken down cottage.Over the years Ears Mouse had made this house a very cozy place and it even had a fireplace and chimney to heat the house in the winter and to boil a little pot of water to make his favorite drink – nettle leaf tea.The old Oak tree that Ears Mouse lived under was also the home to one of Ears Mouse's friend, Sam Squirrel. Sam's house was a hole about halfway up the tree where a large branch had dropped off a few years ago during a terrific gale. When it broke off it had left a hole into part of the tree, which had died about fifty years ago when it had been hit by lightning. This had left a hollow in the dead part of the tree and had made an excellent place for a house. There was lots of room for Sam to be able to store his hazel nuts each year before the winter set in. There were lots of other trees in Pine View forest and there was nothing that Sam enjoyed more than jumping from tree to tree in search of more nuts. He was vary daring and if you saw him jump you would sometimes think he had wings as he would appear to fly from one branch to another. Next door to Ears Mouse's house was a very big house which belonged to his friend Jerry Jermie. Harry's house was not quite as tidy as Ears Mouse's house as he was always picking up bits of grass and leaves on his spikes and then bringing them into his house where they would fall onto the ground. However it was a very cozy house with a lovely carpet of soft straw which made you feel like you were floating on air. Jerry Jermie was very proud of his garden where he grew some very tasty vegetables. He never had any problems with slugs or grubs, which would normally make holes in the vegetables, as they were his favorite type of food.

The next building along road was more of a pool rather than a home. Here stayed Dezzie Frog who became the greatest sprinter among all lane-living species. He is also the greatest and fastest jumper, that proved useful to get there quick. Dezzie used to stay underneath a big daisy plant at the bottom of a lake which was like his shades to block out the sun. He will leap out of the pool throughout the day and run though the tall grass throughout the pasture area of peasant Gill in search of bugs lying on the mossy rocks. He will eat any kind of bug he might catch but he enjoyed blue flies particularly since they were so tasty.

Only a bit later on was fellow Louise with Ears Cat. Hammy was probably the best buddy of Ears Mouse since they had matured with each other and both enjoyed a lot of the same stuff like cheese and grain. Hammy had a really comfortable room, but since it was lined with straw that was just as Hammy wanted to be, this was difficult to go into. That kept it a really pleasant home throughout the year, even throughout the coldest temperatures. He would open his front door and then climb into the straw and vanish and if you tried to draw his attention, you just had to yell loudly. Throughout the day Louise was a fitness fanatic, he'd sit near the line of traffic for hours to ensure he didn't put on that much poundage – because he would never fit in to his apartment if he appears to have done.

After that was Lucy Mole whose room, because the gate became flat on the floor, was indeed a bit strange. Lucy stayed deep underground and now once more pushed her home across the road, starting a new doorway every moment. She won't have very poor vision or just a very nice sense of balance, which supposed she ran into stuff once in a while and had an achy nose. She never went too far but she was only a little bit small and that was hard to reach beneath the dirt. Lucy usually came out only at dark, and if she ever went out all day she would almost hold her eyelashes shut to shield her delicate eyes against getting sunshine.

Lastly, Ears Mouse's best pal Suzaine Owl stayed just within the Pine View tree. Suzaine was housed in a really tall elm tree that was one of the tallest plants present. She typically took a nap, and only headed out to eat when it was dusk. Suzaine was a really special Owl since she was a vegan and had spared Ears Mouse from ever being killed by some other Owl, in which he was only a mouse for kids. He had already been running with his mom as it was getting dark and not seeing behind the form of a massive owl. Before the owl got to Ears Mouse Suzaine Owl barged or brought him home and dropped him next to his mum. The mom of Ears Mouse had never seen anything like this, nor felt she wouldn't see Ears Mouse ever. They also expressed their gratitude to Suzaine Owl and have become good friends.

Ears Mouse had several other colleagues, all of whom were Drip Donkey, that crossed the path now and then again. Drip stayed in the farm but at the other part of Peasant Gill's shed but when it was time to harvest he generally helped push the harvest cart out. Often Drip will come down the pitch seeing his buddy if anyone had left the gate opened to his area.

The Picnic Ahhhhhhh – Ears Mouse released a really long breath and raised his arms after he awoke today. He got up, put on his bathrobe and headed on to the opening for the shades to open. And once he raised his shades, he saw the sun rising, but to his shock the horizon was entirely black with no cloud in view. He gave a massive smile, because that was just what he was doing. This was just the perfect day for a lake-side picnic he figured for sure.

Ears Mouse consumed his cereal as quickly as he can and, when doing a shower and at same time pushing ready. He would be out the gate under no moment and he makes his way across the lush green road to his mates' homes. He then call in at the house of Jerry Jermie. 'Jerry,' Ears Mouse yelled, scratching at his door, 'you've seen how beauuuuuuu. It's tiful now and great for a pond picnic? Jerry cautiously opens his eyes still partially shut, already in his pyjamas. As he was so vivid that was he have to roll his eyes and went straight back home to grab his shades.

'Wow,' Jerry Jermie said, 'yeah, great conditions for an Ears Mouse picnic, I'll be prepared right away.' His closest colleagues, Dezzie Rat, Louise , Lucy Mole and Sam Squirrel, headed in seeing Ears Mouse instead. Everyone decided that only a picnic was a great idea, and planned to meet in half hour at Ears Mouse's place.

Ears Mouse immediately went back to his home, making some good chocolate sticks and a half of an apple that he would have picked that day in an apple tree. The slices tasted so good that he had been almost compelled to instantly eat it all. He put all his food wisely in his backpack and got his wool beanie hat then headed outside for a while in line to have all his buddies arrive at his house.

'Prepared? 'Ears Mouse asked, 'Up,' then everyone replied, so they went through the farms to Woodside Lake, some of the beloved picnic places. As it seems, Woodside Lake was really nearby to the forest named Woodside but was in which Suzaine Owl, another friend of Ears Mouse, stayed. Ears Mouse understood Suzaine was going to be sound asleep at such a time of day because she was staying up most of the night so needing her bed, so he didn't ask her if she wished to go out to the party for such a purpose.

Woodside lake wasn't that far away but Lucy Mole was a little sluggish and her vision in the daylight wasn't so nice. Thus Sid Squirrel had her rest almost all of the way on his neck. On the route they all conversed about certain wonderful times they got last season at Woodside Lake. They reached at the reservoir after around nearly an hour then Jerry Jermie laid a large kilt blanket over the surface. Each of them laid their backpacks on the ground, then brought their beverages outside and put them in a nearby pond that flowed into the lake to hold them cold. It was too soon to start feeding and that they all goes down to the lakeside then threw their heads across the edge and through the water – all that apart from Dezzie Frog who jumped right in with a huge plunge in.

Dezzie vanished for a few moments below the waters but suddenly reappeared on his head with a wide smile – 'mind-blowing' he said, 'come on, it's about the perfect temperature.' Even the participants rolled their eyes, none of those could dive, and they won't even want to get soaked with the exception of their foot, or even when they needed to shower.

They both felt a little woozy for a moment, and ran back to the picnic blanket. Ears Mouse pulled out his waffles from his lunch stall and had a quick whiff while taking a chunk – Mmmmmmm, that tastes wonderful he stated. Sid Squirrel had carried several red currants during winter which he had left over. Louise used to have some nice grain which he had picked in the hay field of Rancher Gill the week before. Jerry Jermie had delivered several grubs that he have picked up that day - 'good new delicious ones' that he said to himself. Dezzie Frog hadn't had to bring any food, because he picked plenty of bugs along the lake's rim and was nearly finished before the others began feeding.

Ears Mouse stared at Lucy Mole then found that she felt a bit ashamed. Lucy had a very vivid imagination as well as poor vision, and had neglected to carry some milk. All others proposed 'Do you want some of our fresh produce?.' 'No, thanks so much,' Lucy Mole replied, there's only one thing that I want to consume and this is insects. 'My caterpillars resemble worm,' Jerry Jermie said. 'Ugh, how do you consume such awful things,' Lucy Mole replied, 'shameful – good thanks, I have to go to find some new worms.' Then Lucy started digging a pit, something she had been very effective at doing, and she had vanished beneath the earth in no time. Here, Lucy was really weak at the others and it was guidance, sadly. She digged really quickly then dove headfirst for the water.

There has been a very loud hissing sound and then a huge water pipe shot out from where Lucy Mole had begun digging the pit. Everybody glanced around when a drinking fountain fired up into the sky then they realized it was just on surface of the water gun- it was Lucy Mole'Help, help-get me back from there, hurry, I can't bear pressures or water,' Lucy said. 'What are we doing' retorted Mouse of the Ears? 'We may try and stop the liquid apart,' Sid Squirrel retorted. 'We might do,' Dezzie Frog answered, 'so after that, without a major bounce, Lucy will fall would be really upset at us.' 'Fix, assist,' Lucy Mole screamed out once again. All others yelled 'we are trying to think.''Think faster please,' Lucy Mole said, 'I get really damp over here.'

When it was over the sky changed, and a darkness fell over them both, like a storm. Swhooosh, Lucy vanished from those in the rim of the pool. It was Suzaine Owl that flew in Pine View forest from her shrub as well as pulled down, softly picking up Lucy Mole in her clutches.

Suzaine put Lucy Mole softly on the outdoor rug, and afterwards perched nearby. "Suzaine" Ears Mouse stated, "Why are you here? I figured at this moment of day you'd be deep asleep.' 'I was enjoying a really good night,' Suzaine explained 'before I realized Lucy Mole's screaming so I decided I'd best know whatever was going on.' 'Thanks Suzaine,' Lucy said, 'and you're sorry to get up.' 'I might as well get anything to eat now i'm up,' Suzaine added. And everybody gives Suzaine some of the food for a picnic.

They wanted to play a game of tag because they had just finally eaten the meal. Dezzie accepted not to disappear in the water, Sid decided not to climb a mountain, Suzaine accepted not to go in the skies so Lucy decided not to get under the field, particularly while she was still dripping off and didn't want to break up at the peak of a well. They all had a wonderful time searching for each other it'sn't long when they all got wiped out and chose to take a sunny sleep. The sunlight began to set at first and then Ears Mouse feel it's time to begin their way back home. They assembled the picnic, and headed back to the apartment of Ears Mouse through the plains. Suzaine Owl kept Lucy Mole in her paws and fortunately due to her weak vision, Lucy did really not see that far she was flying.

As they all returned to the apartment of Ears Mouse he welcomed them in for pizza as well as tea. They spoke of the great day they had as well as the silly stuff which had occurred for years, or even Lucy Mole felt her trip on tops of the waterfall may have looked weird. They had loved the beautiful lake picnic and were now thinking forward to see more.

3.13.   The Glittery Easter's Eggs

There was once a family who had worked on a dairy. They didn't make ends meet. Whenever the farm starts earning money it seemed many crops might be destroyed or several animals might catch a disease.

Joe & Louise had been the farm owner's daughter & son, Mr. Patrick.

An early Easter dawn, Joe & Louise played down the stream near the field. They were looking for rocks that would carry them away to the creek to seek to avoid the river. This has been most preferred pastimes. Joe looked around an ancient tree's base, As he saw a small white bunny. The rabbit went in a hole, and was gone. Joe & Louise waited about for an hour for the bunny, but he did not come out from his burrow.

When they were almost close of finding rocks to jump into the sea, they found a basket which was green and bright full of sweets and eggs which were golden lying in the base of the huge exanimated tree log. They rushed over, then picked up the tub. They raced home and showed that to their brother.

Mr. Patrick was seated on the porch and he was on the front side with depressed facial expressions, as they got back to the house. All its crops seemed to have ruined this year again. He wasn't a good shepherd.

Mrs. Patrick said: "Hi guys. What was it you were you up to? We were searching for skipping rocks down by the stream and we noticed this tub," Anna said. "What's in same a basket?" Mr. Patrick inquired. "Some dumplings, some golden chickens," Joe said. "Looks like a pretty interesting material," Mr. Patrick said. "Did you suppose it put Easter's Bunny here for you? He inquired the Kids. He was pretending to be interested although he was disappointed at the prospect of going back to the city and finding a factory job. He has always hated life in the area. This is why 3 years earlier, he actually decided to move back to the farmland to try his luck at agriculture.

"You may take brunch for the kids?" Mr. Patrick inquired. "Yes, we're really starving," Joe said. "Let's see what mum wants to cook for lunch," Mr. Patrick said.

They went home, and noticed some new bread made by Mrs. Patrick. "Freshly baked bread, delicious," Louise said. "Do you want any sandwiches, guys?" Then Mrs Patrick inquired. "It sounds terrific to me," Joe said. "And me too," Anna said.

As they started to eat sandwiches the phone bell rang it was Mr Devy, the person in charge of running the bank in locality. He told he had to come along & get several funds from Mr. Patrick to compensate on the farm for the loan that he had.

"What is it we should do? Mr. and Mrs. Patrick confronted one another. They realized they hadn't got the cash that Mr. Devy wished they'd obtain. "I guess we're about to auction the property," Mr. Patrick said.

"Maybe we should send any of the Easter basket golden eggs to him," Joe said. "What sort of basket of Easter?" Then Mrs. Patrick inquired. This got Mr. Patrick's eye because he figured Mrs. Patrick was the individual who that place the Easter basket in the farms that the kids find. "Come on have a glance at those shells," Mr. Patrick said. Joe & Louise went up to the porch and took the container out. Their mother and father stared at the shells. Every picked up one. They'd been enough strong as gold, Mr. Patrick figured. Would they have been gold?

They accomplished to offer Mr Devy one egg in exchange for loan payment which was due on the fields. They knew that he should ask whether or not the egg were genuine gold, because it was believed that Mr. Devy understood between the quality of original gold and false gold.

They rang the doorbell. It was Devy, Mr. All became apprehensive. Will he approve of their egg offer? Will the egg become real gold?

"Hi Mr. Devy," Mr. and Mrs. Patricksaid as Mr. Devy walked through the threshold. "Hey people. I'm sorry I had to be here to ask for support, "Mr Devy said. Everyone suspected that he was not telling the truth.

"I don't have to compensate you with some money but I will sell you those magnificent eggs which are made of gold," Mr. Patrick said. "One golden shell. Are you mad? There is nothing exist which we may call a golden egg, "Mr. Devy said. Everybody seemed concerned.

"I'm asking you what," Mr. Devy said, "provide me the egg & I will bite it in & let you know if it has some original gold present in it." If it has some gold, I'll send you the gold worth of your pocket. "Mr. Patrick gave the egg to Mr. Devy. Mr. Devy held it in his hand, bringing it close to his lips. He fucks the shell. The pupils, as he was, seemed bigger and clearer than anybody else had before. "It's just gold!" Mr. Devy said, seems really enthusiastic. Where did you bring it to in the world? "We had it in basket from Easter," Joe & Louise said with a wide grin on their lips.

"I'm going to send you one thousand dollar cash for that," Mr. Devy said, realizing its worth even much greater than this. "This is a contract," Mr. Patrick said. It would absolutely pay back my debt and give everyone some more money to enjoy. "Everybody in the Patrick family was really pleased as they realized they had a bowl full of golden eggs.

The farm became classified as Luckiest Farms in lieu of Patrick Farms from this day forward.

Each Easter the Patrick's using quite a bit of fortunately discovered riches to put all the I children of their locality in the town down by the stream for a yearly Easter egg hunting.

They weren't fortunate enough to have another golden eggs basket full although they still look like the basket tale with the Easter eggs of gold isn't just a legend, it's real.

3.14.   WATER IN THE DESERT

Once, a boy was raised in a family called Bodhisatva, baptized Vaishya. The family has had a thriving business. When Bodhisatva grew older, he began to assist in the family company. Often he had to travel to other cities to search for water in the desert for company. When Bodhisatva and some five hundred entrepreneurs went on a business tour, we all had their carts of the bullock. The leader cart was leading upfront, and others followed him. The caravan came gradually to the mountains. None to be seen everywhere but sandy desert. After traveling such a long distance through the desert, they all felt exhausted. It was impossible to go on since the sun was too bright.

Seeing all of this, the caravan leader said, "Let's stop here for the day. We'll start our trip in the evening, and then the conditions will be pretty good." They parked their carts in bullock, gave the bulls fodder and water, and went to rest. The caravan leader yelled out in the evening, "O guys get ready for the ride. They're not that far out. We're going to get there in the morning."

Everyone got ready, and one after the other Bullock carts made a long queue. Weight reduction on the bullock carts. They drained the vessel of water to fill the containers with fresh water in the area. They were hoping there would be no more land. Bullock cart caravans continued forward. The carts had accompanied each other tightly. The chief led the caravan into town. Throughout the night, they continued their journey into the dark without realizing whether it was in the right direction or not.

At dawn, they realized they'd lost their way. After a long trip, they finally agreed to go back to the very same spot. As the caravan searched for the place, the sun was getting hotter. They finally reached the same spot where they had been the previous day. The water they brought given them has already been cast out. Already getting so hungry, they searched desperately for water but could not be found anywhere. The carts were stopped in a loop. They 'd died because of cold. Seeing no other option, Bodhisatva agreed to dig across the desert for water. He had been so determined he needed to drill a water well. But his quest continued in vain. Then he began searching for an suitable location where water could be discovered on digging. He went ahead, and discovered some cactus. It occurred to him that it was an appropriate place to dig, as cactus would not grow without underground water. He then told a cart owner, "Mate, dig over here. Water would possibly be found at this location." He started digging. His spade hit a rock when he digged deep! He quit digging and yelled, "There's a block!" Bodhisatva saw the digger, and went down into the hole. He 'd moved back to the block. Suddenly its lights were glowing. Beneath the rock he could detect a rush of motion.

He went out of the pit then said to his companions, "If we don't do anything, we're sure to die of thirst. I've heard water running underneath the rock. Let's try to break the rock at any cost. We 're sure to get water. We're going to have power and courage. Let's try again with confidence." Bodhisatva was saddened to see that none of them had the bravery to go forward to search. Suddenly a young man stood up and managed to pick up the spade, and went down the pit. Seeing the Bodhisatva youth was optimistic for water. At last they found the water in the desert. The youth started to strike the stone with all his strength and the destroyed and a small, pleasant water fountain came up. Seen this, the crowds ran toward the fountain and started joyfully dancing. They quenched hunger. Bulls were given water, too. Both of them praised Bodhisatva, and went on their way. They soon reached the town. Thus Bodhisatva could save the lives of his friends with his courage and determination. In addition, the water fountain was a spot for the tourists to quench their thirst and relax. Strength and bravery are the key to success.

3.16. WATER IN THE DESERT

His wife once worked a woodcutter. He used to cut and sell wood in the mountains. It was the only way of his lifespan—a woodcutter chopping wood. One day, he went to destroy forest timber. On the road, he sang a poem, praising nature and beauty. He noticed a really large tree before him. He figured chopping the entire tree for more timber. As the tree was growing, the wood from it will be enough for his entire life. As the woodcutter picked up his axis to cut the tree, he heard a voice, "Please don't cut this tree." The woodcutter stopped to look but found none. He figured it's an idea. Again he picked his axis and aimed at the tree, but again he heard the same words, "Please be kind to me. Don't cut this tree." The woodcutter stopped and looked around. But he could see none. He was perplexed. And a fairy talked from the tree, "I am a fairy and reside in this tree. I stay in the root throughout the winter, and I reside on the roots during the remainder of the year. When you kill this tree, I would be poor, winter is quickly coming, and I will die of cold. Please don't ruin my house. Then, I will satisfy your three wishes." Now he could be rich without any work. He welcomed the bid of the fairy and rushed home to inform his wife about it. His wife awaited him as well. She was shocked to see the woodcutter back too early and asked, "Why did you come too early today? You 're looking so excited. What's the matter? Please let me know." The woodcutter responded, "I've got a huge fortune today. I 'm going to get the fortune shortly." His wife couldn't understand anything, saying, "What's the matter? Tell me. I can't hold my patience anymore." The woodcutter portrayed his companion. His wife hopped joyfully. The woodcutter said, "I'm starving. Give me anything to eat." His wife said, "Because you arrived late, I haven't cooked something till now. Wait, I'll only prepare anything for you." The woodcutter said, "No, don't cook something. I can satisfy any three wishes. Now, as the first, I want candy and hot pudding." He ate to his enjoyment, loading the plate again and again. Then he begged his wife to finish the pudding. Yet she became really mad, claiming, "You've lost one blessing, and now I want the pudding to be placed on your nose!" The pudding quickly stuck to his nose. The woodcutter got angry and said, "Oh, what a fool you 're! What did you do?" He attempted to clean the pudding from his nose, but the pudding kept trapped. He scolded his wife and said, "You've lost the second blessing, so we should call for loads of revenue." The woodcutter got annoyed, so replied, "God, you 're a huge fool. There's hot pudding sticking to my nose, and you're looking for money! I wish my nose's pudding will disappear instantly!" The woodcutter breathed satisfaction. The woodcutter and his wife wasted the golden chance to become wealthy. Their luck would have knocked at their gate, but the opportunity was missed and remained poor as before.

3.17.   The Ugly Duckling

The tale starts at a field in which a duck sits on an egg clutch to help them hatch. One after another, the eggs start to hatch, and then there will be 6 yellow-feathered ducklings, singing in excitement. The last egg needs longer to develop, and a weird duckling with black feathers grows from it. All, including his mum, considers the grey feathered duckling disgusting. The sad duckling tries to get away and stays in a marsh by itself before winter arrives. When a farmer sees the duckling hungry in the winter, he takes mercy on the poor duckling and offers him food and protection at home. The duckling, though, scares the loud children of the family and flees across an icy lake towards a cave. A herd of stunning swans descends on the lake as spring arrives, and the small duckling, now well grown but alone, reaches to the swans, hoping that he will be rejected. But a big shock! He is greeted by the swans. He looked at his own reflection into the water and realizes he is no longer an ugly duckling but a pretty swan. The swan decides to join that flock and flutters off along with a new and lovely family.

3.18.   The Boy Who Cried Wolf

The narrative comes from the Fables of Aesop, which impresses on the value of being real. It's the tale of a shepherd boy who saw herd of sheep near to his village. The region was reported to have a wolf notorious for attacking the herd of sheep and doing away with a hundred goats. Every villager knew about the threat and was always willing to help anyone who had a trouble. But the boy ignored, and in turn mocked, this friendly aspect of the villagers. He pulled out the villagers for his entertainment, three times, by pleading for support, saying "Bear! Man, dog! ". He was quickly supported by the ever-vigilant farmers, only to see the shepherd boy enjoying a good laugh. They were obviously offended when he chuckled at them for having them tricked. However, one day a wolf actually came and started killing his sheep and eating them. None of the villagers came to his assistance this time when he screamed for support, because they assumed he was playing a joke on them again. As a result the wolves killed the flock of the farmer. The morale of the tale is that, no-one trusts a liar even though he says the truth.

3.19.   Little Albert and White Fluffy Bunny

Little Albert is a baby. He's got one mate, Richard. Robert is a fuzzy white rabbit. His eyes are red and wonderful like flame, his fur white and fluffy like snow, soft and cozy like a bed hugging.

Little Albert and Robert are great mates, they play together all day, they feed together and they sleep together. There's one evil man, though, his name is Dr. Watson. Dr. Watson is a bad guy, and to k ids he's pretty much evil. He said to his mates, "Let's catch up with 12 guys, I can turn them into anything."

Dr Watson went to the garden one day, and little Albert played in the orchard with Robert. Dr. Watson stared at little Albert and said, "Look at this kid and his bunny buddy, they look so joyful, I'm going to make him scared of this rabbit," Dr. Watson made a pit, and sadly little Albert was caught. Robert has been worried and had been wants to assist out. But Dr. Watson helps make a scary sound whenever Robert approaches little Albert. The tone was so terrifying that Robert was terrified away and little Albert busted in tears.

It has been occurring over and over and little Albert became afraid of Bob. Little Albert cries and breaks in anger every time Robert enters, even when Dr. Waston has already departed.

Robert wanted to console little Albert again, but little Albert screamed, "Go ahead, I 'm scared of you, just go now."

Robert was really angry, but he was also eager to support little Albert. So Robert went out to the street, sneaked into the house, and discovered Jerry, a fuzzy rodent, in the house corner.

Robert asked, "Jerry, little Albert, you can help, he's scared of me."

Happily Jerry decided. Then Jerry went to the garden and attempted to console little Albert, but little Albert always cried, "Go away, please go away, I 'm scared of you, you're fuzzy."

Jerry has always been angry. And Robert and Jerry went to the roof and discovered a white cat called Tom. "Tom, you should help little Albert, he's frightened of me," Robert said. Tom enthusiastically accepted. So Tom went to the garden and wanted to console little Albert, but little Albert again pleaded, "Go away, please go away, I 'm scared of you, you're dark."

Robert discovered that little Albert isn't only frightened of him; he's terrified of something like him, so Robert's got a different concept. Robert went to the living room, and discovered old Tony, a hound dog, in his armchair. "Yeah, let me help you" was glad to support old Tony. Old Tony went to the garden, and the little

Albert approached. "Don't be afraid, I'm going to help you," said old Tony in a calm voice.

"I'm not frightened of you, you're not white nor fuzzy," this time little Albert didn't whine.

Old Tony guided little Albert out of the hole, "You are all right now, go and play with your mates, little Albert"

"No, they're too scary," is terrified little Albert. "Little Albert, they're not frightening, they're your friends, they support you," said old Tony, smiling at Robert, Tom and Jerry.

"Ph.D. we're going to protect you, Watson is gone.

Little Albert listened to the words of old Tony and surmounted his fear, he is no longer afraid of his friends.

3.20.   A Queer Friendship

His closest mates were Max puppy and Lucy crow. Yet it was a strange relationship, because Max was deaf and Lucy boring. Lucy did not fly after injuring her left arm and hip, which had been smashed beneath the wheels of a motorcycle. She stood on Max 's back all day and the dog brought her to areas where food was available, including the waste bins and parks on the countryside.

The two mates in the business were content and enjoyed each other and appreciated each other.

The other animals in the community always loved and also welcomed this Queer relationship. But, one day, with the arrival of the monsoons, tragedy hit. The entire field was overflooded. As a consequence, all people and livestock perished, homes ruined and crops burned. Sick and cold, Lucy and Max wanted to quit the city, heading to a new location. Having to carry Lucy on his back, Max trudged along the lane, and only paused to rest at night.

They finally moved to a new place, where the inhabitants were wealthy and food was still polluted with dustbins and roadsides. Max and Lucy both agreed to stay, making it their permanent house. We were happy but not the others. The two men were angry. Leo a street dog called Max a idiot and said, "You're a mad dumb guy." How else would you be wearing the lame crow on your back? Which use would you make of the

Worthless bird? "Lucy was branded a worm by Chinni sparrow and rebuked her for taking advantage of a vulnerable deaf puppy. The locality's crows did not speak to Lucy because she chose to be nice with Max instead of their business. The street dogs for their part ignored Max, as he had lowered himself by holding company with a local crow.

Max just smiled as he learned all this so Lucy was sad. "She thought, I'm worthless." "I just let Max do it all for me, but I never did anything at all for him, nor did I support him in some way." As the days went by Lucy was steadily sad. "I have to do everything for Max to remind him I value him so much and enjoy his friendship."

One day Max was staying on one side of the lane, it was afternoon. Lucy, who sat near Max, instantly spotted a large meat bone from the butcher's shop on the opposite side of the street that had fallen on the ground. Her eyes gleamed. "Let me bring Max the slice of meat. Assuming so, she walked across the ground and pulled her left knee. Bending picked up the slice of bone with her beak and crossed the path when she noticed a vehicle coming at high pace to serve left and right. She even saw Max turning in his sleep and now, stretching halfway across the lane. "I've got to alert him." Lucy was panicking, and wondering. Acting on an whim, at Max, Lucy tossed the bone with all her strength. Startled, Max opened his eyes and looked up at the car. Instantly behaving, he jumped over to safety.

Lucy had rescued Max's career, and now all the animals and birds were starting to value Lucy.

3.21. DINOSAURS IN MY BED

Andrew lay in his room, shivering. Only beyond his house, the sky was filled with loud noises and bright lights.

He asked fifteen minutes ago, "Mother, will the tempest last long?"

"Don't stress please," she added. "The weatherman said Truro would easily cross through. Have more relaxation now.

Except that they didn't; so he couldn't.

Andrew saw his alarm clock. "Tick ... Tick ... Tock." Evidently the night lasted indefinitely. Seconds give way to minutes.

And for what seemed as hours. Loud lightning bolts over the house caused him crawl deeper under the covers. His glass also rang out noise.

Does he have to move into his parent 's room? But now, he was a big kid. And he has had to be courageous. Father helped him prepare for that poor weather.

It lasted the whole night just in case. Now he'd covered my bag under the covers. Made with childhood gadgets, cards, and comic books. He 'd already seen "Panda" bear when he was two years old.

Mom made sure there were a few treats for Andrew too. On his right hand was a large bag of popcorn. Then on the other, there was one packet of rippled chips.

His family was tenting last weekend in Cape Breton. And instead, he was a kid with experience camping. stYet he had learned how to stay brave.

Which jumped on the toes? "Ouch that hurt," whispered his shivering voice. There was a much noise outside Andrew could hardly speak.

A dim night filtered the stars out of the glass.

The kid immediately became excited. What was the pillow beneath? He's been wondering, rummaging in his bag.

"OMIGOSH!" said Andrew. "I just forgot about my torch."

He rolled out of bed, and ran across the floor. Andrew searched about in the top dresser drawer before he discovered it.

Jumping back into bed easily, he pulled freezing feet down to the very edge. Bare toes laid loosely on something hard. Now it seemed to creep around his ankles. Yikes ... Yikes! He hadn't been in bed yet!

He looked under the coverings where it was black as tar, just as outside. Rather of showing up gleaming stars, highlights appeared much like eyes.

From behind his left knee came Roaring. Andrew chewed at his left hand, looking at the torch. "It couldn't be that scary sound ...? "He wavered.

Yeah, you dinosaur! Yet that was unlikely, was it not? Dinosaurs couldn't fit beneath a little boy's bedcovers, residing within his room. Exactly right?

Incorrect. This was a Stegosaurus to star right at him. Then they tried his vinegar chips from Hostess, the only little packet left only a few morsels.

"Go your way, you! "Andrew bellowed, then attempted to be courageous. Someone rumbled back underneath the blanket-sky and dashed into a dark corner.

New sounds catched the eye of the child. His flashlight helped pick out shadows that were moving. What happened? He marvelled. A Triceratops and a Deinonychus were in there.

And another Tyranosaur!

"Start off! "Andrew yelled. Instantly he felt as if he were the only one on earth alive. But he was still under his blanket, which appeared to be expanding in the distance and even above him.

He was searching for places to run.

Cold feet just couldn't move. Beneath the blankets it was like another world. His core marched to drum rhythm. Lightning zipped then zapped beneath his cloak.

Large animals had started chasing smaller ones.

Racing a Dicraeosaurus toward him. It was a friendly eater of plants that did not harm him. But, Andrew was not able to take any chances.

He took his bag off a fire truck. Jumping on the front seat, Andrew turned the siren to maximum power. All he did was ears hurt.

An Albertosaurus and Ceratosaurus bounded after him. We were like those big nice dogs that liked to play. But Andrew hadn't wanted to get crushed. He pushed on the throttle button. And the fire engine sprang forward. The road soon became a narrow lane, led straight into the trees. Andrew parked fast. Then he laced his backpack on new sneakers. He brought in his whistle, too. Shrill blowing warned us all to get out of his way. A flurry of feet fled down the trail, pounding hard at every step. One arm clung straight to 'Panda.'

The wind blew off his cap and sent it down the road. Branches to his neck grabbed. He did not want any dinosaurs to be squashed or eaten. Compared to the wild animals following him under his blanket, the storm outside was nothing. Why did it all happen anyhow? Growls and feet speeding kept focus behind him. Reaching Andrew grabbed his roller blades into his backpack. Now, he figured, Skating away safely should be fast. That is, before he was driven to the mud by a sly tree root. Now it was time to climb a tree in a hurry. "Mom, where are you? "Andrew screamed. "Daddyyyy! " Skinny legs were scrambled the trunk. And like a monkey, from branch to branch climbed up higher.

The head of a Brontosaur was unexpectedly between two arms. Smiled as he chewed a leafy mouthful. "What is your problem with that? "It seemed to be said. "Andrew, ANDREWW! "someone shouted. Voices were like waves going back and forth, running around. Yes, his name was shouted by the people!

The boy hurriedly threw his blankets off, sat up, and stared at his mother and father. He gazed in between Venetian blinds while the morning sun peeked. "Panda" was now tucked under his arm, safely. "Beneath your blankets I see you found our surprises," Mom said. Andrew stared at his mother blankly.
"You know. Do you remember the dinosaur models that you have asked last week?"

"I'm proud of you," daddy said. "see how tidily you set them all on your dresser."

When dad found out, Andrew looked strange. A group of vibrant dinosaurs stood in a tidy row. We chased a sweet Dicraeosaurus, and at the end of the line a fearsome looking Tyrannosaurus Rex. Leading the party as a whole was a little boy guy. So he hugged closely to a teddy bear.

Both the dinosaurs in this Fantasy story are accurately named. My wife, Esther and I have visited Drumheller in the area of Calgary Alberta where they roamed once.

3.22.   WOODY THE WOODPECKER

Julie hen went to the house of her aunt Mira located at the end of wood.   She had told her good friend Diana duck to take care of her Gigi baby before she left. It was a dozing afternoon when small Gigi stepped out into the daylight from underneath the wings of the duck and started catching bugs.The fox named Johnny, who'd been awaiting for such a golden chance for several days, and particularly that day, because he knew Gigi 's mother was trapped in his tight grip by the chick. However he noticed his name was being called from far before Johnny could feast on Gigi. It was Sam fox his buddy who came to visit him. Johnny said to himself, "I would not like to share you with others." He placed Gigi in a box placed in front of his house, banging the door.

Woody the woodpecker observed the hearings seated on a rock, and heard the cry of pain from the chicken. 'In the wooden shell, the poor creature will die of oxygen deprivation,' thought Woody. After Johnny had gone to visit his buddy Sam, Woody flew from the tree, seated on the crate, and with his beak created holes on it. Air began to flow in the box and Gigi could breathe again.

Meanwhile, Diana duck in Gigi 's quest learned of the entire Roma butterfly incident, and Tuna porcupine, Ruby Giraffe, all had learned of Gigi 's troubles. This is Charlie monkey strutting from one tree to the other who first tried to enter the wooden box and pull the lid open. Julie hen was joined with Gigi on her comeback and she was very thankful to Woody the Woodpecker, without his help and effective treatment, her child would have expired. Henceforth the two were best friends.

Fearing of the animals' vengeance, Johnny decided to leave the jungle for better.

3.23.   The Teddy Bear War

"I am the most slim! "And Baxter Bear asked Billy Bear. He was definitely a beautiful teddy bear. His hair was light gray, and he was sporting a black jumper and a cap with straw.

"I am the most slim! "Insisted by Billy Bear. He was a very pretty teddy bear too. His hair was gray with snow and he put a red jumper over his sweet teddy bear face with little glasses.

We stood on Cindy's bunk. The little girl liked them a lot, and took good care of them still. Per day, she washed them clean with a fluffy cloth and adjusted their sweaters all the way. At night she had them sleep with her in the tent. Every Saturday afternoon she had a tea party for them. She also brought them with her to Grandma's while she was about to play.

After quite some time the two teddy bears were happy with this plan. They both recently felt maybe one would be stronger than the other.

"The way you do, I don't wear yucky lenses," Baxter told Billy, as they relaxed on the bed and wait for Cindy to come back home from kindergarten.

"The way you do, I don't carry a dumb straw hat," Billy commented.

"Wait" said Baxter. "When Cindy gets home from school she'll wake me up first and kiss me. She does so still.'

"No, she isn't," he told Billy. "I am the one who she still picks up first and kisses."

"We are going to talk about it," said Baxter.

"We'll think about that," Billy said. They stayed together on the bed waiting for Cindy to come home. They stayed all afternoon on the fuzzy pink couch and didn't utter a thing to each other. They had been best mates at one point but now they were in the midst of a battle to see who was the slenderest. Everyone thought it was him. Cindy had plenty of toys and dolls but her favorites had always been Baxter and Billy. She received them from her grandpa, who died just before Baxter came to her and Billy did. In reality they were really different.

We remained together in quiet all afternoon and then saw Cindy downstairs. She's been home from college! We saw her come running up the stairs.

"We shall see," muttered Baxter to Billy.

"We shall see," whispered Billy back.

Cindy ran into her bedroom and flung herself down onto her pillow. Her curly pigtails were cute. She had freckles on her cheeks and lost all of her front teeth. When Baxter and Billy placed the teeth under her pillow so the Tooth Fairy might come to see her, she recalled. The Tooth Fairy gave her two cents, and she got Baxter the straw hat and Billy the shoes.

At the same time she picked them both up and hugged them. "What are my two friends doing? "Everyone was granted a kiss on the face. "I've got some wonderful things to say my darlings! My other tooth is loose and that means coming to visit the Tooth Fairy again. I will give you guys, when she does, a sweet little teddy bear bed that you will share with. Mommy says she's going to help me pay for it, because she knows how much I love my children. "I am going to get my milk and biscuits now, darlings. The boys are good and I will come back in a little bit. "She gently set them down on the blanket and rushed downstairs.

Baxter considered Billy. "We both all are special."

Billy looked Baxter. "We're growing just Cindy's cutest teddy bear."

They grinned and rested on the bed waiting for her to finish her snack and returned to play with them.

Chapter 4: Inspirational Bedtime Stories

Milton Erickson believed that every child has a motivating desire to know and explore, that any stimulation is an opportunity for the child to react in a new way (1980), through which we may infer that the purpose of pediatric psychotherapy is to promote and enhance these learning opportunities. Knowing how to read is one of the basic skills in adulthood, equipping the infant with information, exchanging memories, coping mechanisms, purpose, happiness, and living well-being. Our concept of schooling, however, extends beyond the three Rats that are the foundation of our educational programs to involve building on and using the innate interest of the infant and the ability to learn as a framework for the development of beliefs, pro-social habits, problem-solving approaches, and other essential qualities that are incorporated — or not — during childhood.

We also included stories in this chapter about inspiring children to make a change, cultivating optimistic attitudes to life conditions and learning to be self-reliant. There are tales of how to leverage a child's talents, tools, and ability, as well as how to adopt a practical path to happiness (Burns & Lane, 2003; Seligman, 2002).

4.1. Kids can make a difference – Goldilocks and four bears

A long time ago, when Goldilocks visited, there were just three bears. Now there are four — Little Bear, Mama Bear, Big Brother Bear, and Papa Bear. Grandpa Bear had come to live with the Bear family even after Goldilocks' tour. He was a poor old bear whose hair had turned grey. As he attempted to chew, his hands moved, and his head leaned down as if he were sick of standing.

Little Bear cherished dog Grandpa. Grandpa Bear still listened to Little Bear while everyone else was getting too far to gather honey or something. If Little Bear tried to rest peacefully on his lap and be told a story, Grandpa Bear would never tell "No." And there were other fantastic tales about Grandpa Bear.

Grandpa Bear, whose hands rattled so badly at times that his spoon could skip his mouth and spill porridge all over his head, was always sorry for Little Bear too. He will also drop his bowl on the concrete floor, crack the bowl and create a huge mess.

He'd have mother bear and dad bear upset. Besides destroying the all bowls that Goldilocks had made popular in her novel, they had to clean up after him. "As if we don't still have anything to do," they would complain. Big Brother Bear will say something like, "Grandpa Bear has the plague of CRAFT — He Can't Recall a Burning Thing," and laugh loudly. Little Bear realized she was mocking Big Brother Bear but it always hurt and she despised him for it. She tried to support Grandpa Bear so what was she supposed to do?

One day, once again, when Grandpa Bear lost his mug, Little Bear got down on the floor and took all the bits. Afterwards she asked Papa Bear if he had some adhesive.

"Why would you want some glue?" Papa Bear inquired.

"And, after I've grown up, I will tie the bowl of Grandpa Bear back together and hold it for you and mum," Little Bear answered.

Silently, Papa Bear leaned back in his daddy-bear chair and stared at Mama Bear in her mom-bear chair. They both stared at each other for a moment. We became kinder to Grandpa Bear after that, Little Bear said. They got him a special plastic grandpa bowl that wouldn't fall too quickly off the table, and wouldn't crack if he dropped it. When he poured porridge down his hair or created a mess on the tablecloth, they didn't appear to mind too much. We talked more to him, and listened to his stories, even though they had read them before.

And this is a happy conclusion to our plot. Mum Bear and Papa Bear became happy, due to Little Bear. Big Bear Pal. Okay, he was the same as he'd always been. No wonder Grandpa Bear was happy. And Little Bear too was happy.

4.2. Kids can make a difference – Trevor a boy in early teens

Trevor did what a lot of other 13-year-old kids might do that night: he watched tv. He noticed on the television a report of some homeless people living out on the sidewalks in the rain, in a trendy section of Philadelphia where he worked. Trevor never once quit talking about how fortunate he was to stay in the same city's relatively well-to-do neighborhood. His heart was moved by the stories of homeless people and he began asking what he should do to support these men.

Trevor might possibly have known about it. There are so many tragic things you can see on Television. That may have been yet another aspect he overlooked.

Perhaps Trevor felt too, Ok, what should I do with it? I am a child, but he wasn't. Then, he began asking if he could support and this prompted him to recall that there were some unused, spare blankets in their workshop. So he went to his friend, wondering if he could take them to the downtown citizens who had no homes to go to the night.

Maybe Trevor's father thought the request was a bit weird. It's natural for children to try to cling on to the stuff we've got, good for adults to believe they've been working hard to earn what they deserve and why would they offer it away? I suppose it's pretty much the same as a kid thinks, it took me a long time to save my pocket money to help purchase this new ride, so why would I gift it to a buddy who wants to get home quickly?

Now, Trevor's father had been a kind-hearted kid. He rode downtown Trevor to help out some of the residents on the streets with a few leftover blankets. When it came time to curl up and sleep that night, I think the citizens were pretty satisfied with the new blankets providing comfort.

Trevor, too, was pleased. He felt nice to give out the blankets. He sensed an intense fire, almost as though he himself had been enveloped in an emotional blanket. But he knew that there was a risk — it might feel so amazing that you would like to do it again.

Trevor went the next day to his nearby grocery store and other public areas in his area where notice boards were placed. He put up posters asking that citizens contribute whatever extra blankets or food they didn't use. The outcome was outstanding. Kindness was universal. Trevor saw so many people eager to support he packed his father's workshop with food and blankets within a week.

What had started with Trevor's generosity developed and spread across the group? It wasn't long until the kindness of the citizens overflowed from the garage of his father and Trevor and his father needed to search for a better building to accommodate all the presents that were donated. Will you know that there are already a variety of different warehouses all over Philadelphia that store food and blankets to feed and shelter the homeless? They are both named "the place of Trevor."

4.3. Feed what you want to grow – An inspirational bedtime story for kids

A grandfather and his grandson settled down on a rock in the sunlight next to a babbling lake.

"Tell me one story," the grandson said.

"This is a two-wolf tale," Grandfather said. "As we develop it often seems like two wolves are fighting to gain power inside of us. The first wolf with soft gray fur, a loving look in his eyes, and maybe even a friendly smile on his lips, you might imagine. It is a wolf who barely ever bars his teeth and is able to stand back and let feed the little ones. We might name him the wolf of harmony, compassion and goodness, because the wolf believes that if we can work alongside each other in harmony, every animal and every human being would be far happier.

"Love is more important to this wolf than everything else. You see, she thinks our animal and human existence will cease to exist without affection. It's because a mother loves her baby that she takes care of her, cooks her, dresses her, covers her and saves her from danger. We come into the world as an act of affection and we learn from the affection parents give us. If we love and are cherished in exchange, we hope to be accepted, and our souls are nurtured and filled.

"Apparently the wolf always understands that goodness is part of that affection. When we are compassionate to someone they are apt to display compassion back to us, if not always. Smile at someone and they can smile back with a fair chance. Go off to be helpful and the one you are helping is more likely to help you when you need it. Wolves are a little like dogs, who work in packs. They blend together, and usually feel happier when they combine in a dry, harmonious way.

"But," the grandfather added, "lets say that the group includes another wolf that doesn't think the same way. This wolf has a really mean, mischievous face. Often it draws back its lips to threateningly show its teeth against other species. Typically they experience terror more than affection and reverence as it happens, because that is the wolf of anger, greed and hate. Maybe it's afraid or nervous, and so it's just on watch. Unfortunately, it hasn't realized that it creates a lot of negative emotions among itself and in the other wolves by being too frustrated or violent toward others, by thinking about who or what it hates more than who or what it loves. This wolf is looking for number one while the wolf of harmony, compassion, and goodness watches out for the joy and well-being of others as well as for his own.

"As you may guess, there might be two these wolves in a group fighting to see which one is heading off on its path. The wolf of goodwill, compassion, and goodness wishes to express those ideals with everyone, but the wolf of greed, covetousness, and hate cares only about himself. It feels terrible about itself and leaves it feeling worse for those around it.

"Let's carry on dreaming," the grandfather said, "that two such wolves are in a fight inside you." The little boy stared up at his grandparents, wide-eyed. "Which one wins? "He inquired anxiously.

The grandfather looked down, compassion in his eyes, gentleness in his expression, replying, "The one you feed."

4.4. Look after yourself – Five little chickens

Have you heard the story of the Five Chickens? Okay, once in a while there were five little chickens residing alongside Daddy Rooster and Mommy Hen. One morning the five little chickens woke up feeling hungry, as most of us do first thing in the morning or afternoon when we get home from school. The first said, "I'm tired. I wish someone would send me a big fat worm. "He began to think about a big fat worm, he wanted to peck it in his beak and hear it slithering in his gut, as if you were a starving little chicken, I suppose you should. Not quite what I'd want for tea! What's up with you?

No matter how badly anyone might like the first little chicken to send him a big fat worm, no worm came and the hunger he looked.

Even the second little chicken was thirsty, so when she heard her brother speak about a big fat worm, she replied, "I am now famished. I wish there was a huge fat slug here in front of me right now. "In excitement, she stared at the table. She glanced about and stared back. And they got ever more hungry.

The third little chicken, like his brother and girlfriend, felt as hungry. "Cheep, cheep," he said, anticipating that someone might notice. "I wish the farmer would bring us a big bowl of those delicious chicken pellets he sometimes delivers." With that thought in his head he was watching the gate in the coop, hoping the farmer would appear. And felt like he was thirsty.

"And," said the fourth, following her brothers and sisters wishes, "that the farmer's wife should carry out from last night's meal, like she always does, one of those large bowls of food scraps." Like her dad, she stood watching the gate in the coop, hoping and hoping a big bowl of scraps. And grow tired.

All this discussion of food got become ravenously hungry the fifth chicken feeling he felt he was going to faint. "What I would not give for a large crunchy grain tub," he said. "I wish I had some 52 curing tales, maize, oats, or barley teaching tales." His eyes were focused on the tin tray where the farmer often scattered some food. He gazed at the tray and looked away, growing hungry by the second.

Overhearing the desires of the five little chickens, Daddy Rooster said, "Come here." Collecting the five little chickens around him, he said, "Do you see what Mommy Hen and I do when we're hungry? Help us out into the garden patch if you decide to have coffee. You will learn to hack and peck your own food there, much as we do.

4.5. It's in the way you do it – An inspirational bedtime story

One day the breeze, the heat, and the sun spoke about how they should convince us to adjust what they were doing. Often it may be a huge challenge because you are performing something that you just don't want to do, or doing something that don't benefit you or anyone. Yeah, that's what the breeze, rain, and sun is thinking about. "Let's just play a draw," the sun said. "See the man with a jacket over there? Let's see who can convince him to cut it off. "The breeze said enthusiastically," Let me try first. The wind began rushing by the ear of the child, at first softly saying, "Take off your jacket. Take off your jacket. "If the boy didn't take off his jacket, the wind began roaring a bit harder towards his face, but the stronger it screamed, the warmer the boy got, so the more snugly he wrapped around his jacket. The wind in his ear started to hurl harder. It was no longer pressing him for instructions but roaring: "Take off your shirt!

Take the jacket off! "The more the boy defied the breeze screamed the louder. So the more the man overlooked. The wind blew out, screaming and spinning, but the boy snuggled tighter into his blanket, pulling it more closely around his chest.

"Grant me a try," the rain said. "What you're doing clearly isn't effective. There's no use in yelling at him, and the sooner you try, the more he's wearing his sweater. "The rain continued to do what it does best. It started to roar quietly, calling as it dripped through the ears of the kid, "Take off your jacket. Taking off your hat. "But then the boy pulled the cap around his head and zipped the hat to keep out the rain on his body. Frustrated, it was determined the storm should not give up. It seemed to ignore the strong wind advice it had provided. "If he's not going to listen to me, I'm going to beat him to take off his jacket," the rain said angrily, and started pouring heavily with that. Raindrops pelted the boy: "Take your jacket off! Take the jacket off! "But the child declined to listen anyway. The storm changed to hail and flew at him, yelling loudly at him to take his jacket off. Instead, the boy decided to cover whatever aspect of him the jacket was able to conceal and search about, searching for protection to grab.

"It has got to be my time," the sun said softly. It began to shine off, drying the boy and his jacket without saying a word. The sun started caressing the boy in water, only slowly increasing the air temperature without having it too high. The kid slid the hood behind at first. When the sun kept warming the day softly, the kid pulled off his jacket zipper. Carefully, the sun lifted the temperature to another degree or two, all the while caressing the boy warmly, and it wasn't long before the boy stripped out of his sweater to fully appreciate the sunshine's soothing warmth.

4.6. Make the most of what you have been given

Once upon a time there was a farmer not far from a country town, who had a small farm. He owned very little but he was able to support his family from this small farm. Of the few items he had, one had been an elderly mule. The old mule had helped him plow his field for years, bring his produce into the village and push his family to church every Sunday, harnessed to a horse.

The village near where the farmer lived loved to stage all the yearly festivities, and planned to have a fireworks display for the coming New Year. No one stopped to think about how an old mule in a neighboring paddock could impact that.

The mule stood in his paddock, head dropped to the ground, eyes closed, sleeping peacefully on New Year's Eve when unexpectedly the sky filled with odd streaks of light and cannon-like bangs that could have heralded the beginning of a war. Thinking the world was coming to an end, the poor mule fled in panic, racing desperately across the paddock. There was an old well inside the paddock as it occurred. It was empty and neglected, not having been willing to maintain its water flow for several years. The mule would normally have evaded it very carefully. But the mule staggered in the pitch black of the night and was overcome with fear, and dropped the small well. Luckily he arrived at the bottom unharmed.

The farmer was surprised to find his mule missing the next day, and started searching around his house. It wasn't long until he heard a soft, ringing bray coming from the well's depth and finding his mule at the bottom to his dismay. There was no way he could comfortably get to the mule by slipping down the old well. There wasn't a large enough ladder in the village to reach the bottom and how would he get the mule out, even if he'd been able to get down? He called to help his peasant friends. They figured they should set a winch up to lower the farmer down to the mule, but the well's walls were too rusty and decaying. It had been too dangerous. How should he add a brace to raise the mule out of such a limited room, even though they had lowered anyone down?

The farmers sat peering down across the well and rubbed their ears. "That is impossible," one said. "Unthinkable," said another. "He'll probably die a long, horrible death down there," a third said. "Better put him out of his misery." So the farmers picked up some shovels and started to bury the mule by pouring dirt down the well.

The mule noticed this strange stuff, like dry rain, dropping on his back at the bottom of the well; he gave himself a shake, and the dirt dropped through his hooves. The mule staggered a bit, and the dirt beneath its hooves became rough. Further dust was falling down on his legs. He brushed it off, then rolled even more once again. He was shocked to note that the bottom of the well had risen by an inch or two after doing so for a bit. He stood a bit further up at the wall than he had been before. The harder the farmers kicked in the dirt, the more the mule shook it off and trampled it deeply beneath its hooves — and the further it climbed bit by bit upward to the top. Yeah, the mule finally found its way to the brink, as you suspected, and was saved.

4.6. Do what you can do.

It's easy enough to find yourself in turmoil even because you don't want it to be. Often we don't know what to do when we are facing a new situation, probably because we never had to experience it before. That's what got Mrs. Teresa Frog. Everyone had used to name her Little Tessie Tadpole when she was little. She favoured Ms. Teresa Frog now, because she was smaller. Ms. Teresa Frog had been working on a farm in a field. She was an imaginative young frog who loved to go and play. Others characterized her as nosy, or a "sticky beak." She was always told by her mother that she stuck her nose where she should not. "Mark my name," he would say to her mother. "You're going to be in big trouble one day." But Teresa needed to discover. She just wanted to figure out things she didn't know. After all, leaving her pond and going running across the farmyard was enjoyable. Seeing the comical chickens scratching busily and pecking their way through the coop was always enjoyable. She didn't want to be confined much like them, she said to herself.

She had found that almost all visiting the pigpen gave her the ability to catch a plump fly or two. There were so many around her that her long tongue's fast flick almost always ensured a meal. This specific day, after smelling the new scent of milk, Ms. Teresa Frog (formerly known as Little Tessie Tadpole) was running by the dairy. She found the tempting smell coming up from a bucket on the floor after her nose. She climbed to the top of the pot, trying to try the sugar, but did not reach nearly far enough. She tried again, putting all of her effort into this. She overdid it this time, leaping straight over the rim and landing with a soft plop in the lush cream.

The cream was moist, and dense. In her frozen pool it felt so much better than swimming. Perhaps better, drinking had tasted fine. She flicked out her long tongue, and lapped a few rich mouthfuls. But after playing and drinking her fill for a bit, Ms. Teresa Frog felt it was time to go back into her pond house. That was when the trouble began. You know, Ms. Teresa Frog hadn't been looking too far ahead. She would have been thinking about getting into the bucket but she hadn't given any thought to get out of the bucket. The walls were high, her feet coated in cream were too slick for a grip so she couldn't just hop off the top. She was trapped, feeling powerless and knew what to do.

She should just move on, she said to herself. But even though she might have enjoyed herself for a bit, this would not fix her dilemma. She might wait for someone to come and save her, but it might be a long time, so if the farmer found her, he would not be too happy to discover a frog in his cream that had just visited the swimming pigpen. If she surrendered and stopped, she could drown.

Oh my little Ms. Teresa Frog it all felt so rough. She did the only thing she could do, not knowing what to do: She stopped swimming. She swam in the cream round and round, doing the frog jump, as frogs prefer to do. She sat back, then screamed. She sat back, then screamed. She then threw out a couple more. Ms. Teresa Frog has been adamant she will not give up and drown. She had to carry on, so she kicked and kicked a few more. As she did, she began to notice that swimming through the cream was becoming increasingly difficult. She thought she was just getting sleepy at first, but then noticed that the cream itself was getting thicker. Her kicking turned the milk into butter!

In that, her faith was renewed and she swam faster and deeper, going round and round in the bucket until the butter was so strong that she could stand on it and run. Fair over the bucket top. Tired, she joyfully jumped back into the pool. When she washed the butter off her body in the bath, Ms. Teresa Frog said to herself, "I have liked cream but I love butter best.

4.7. Seeking happiness – an inspirational bedtime story for kids

There was once a princess who had it all. Ok, pretty much everything. She lived in a magnificent palace. She was the most significant person in all 58 Healing Tales, Teaching Tales Nation, after the king and queen. She was of course the queen, she had everything she could possibly think of.

Can you work it out? If she wanted it, so all she needed to do was inquire, and she was given it. She was a modern queen, who got the best in new toys. She had a specially designed toy palace packed with dolls from Barbie and Ken, and all their accessories. She had the best in video games played on a huge plasma screen in her playroom, which occupied a whole wall. And her playroom alone was as large as some houses where some of her kingdom's families lived. And she still lost interest, got bored or felt alone amid all of this. The princess will often open her playroom window and gaze out at the streets below. There she saw other kids play hopscotch or tag, laugh, talk and sing. "How do the kids make all those sounds?" The princess one day told her kingly nanny. "I guess that is because they are satisfied," the royal nanny responded.

The princess looked down at the kids again, and said, "I just want to be happy. What are they going to make me happy? "The kingly nanny had never before found herself in such a difficult position. If she could just let the princess out onto the streets to play with the other kids, the princess might start learning to laugh and having fun too. If only the princess had some friends she could share stories with, chat about her thoughts or even do some of the stuff that a friend is good to do. The nanny also started to talk of certain ideas that would have been too evil for a royal nanny to have. She wondered if the princess would like playing a fun snowball battle with other kids on the sidewalks, or if she'd joke about paddling barefoot in the mud along the side of the river and maybe making one of her cute little dresses dirty. How would it be for her not to care about her looks, or what other people were feeling of her? But these were of course not things a royal nanny might tell to the princess and yet keep her work. Besides that, no matter what the nanny thought, the princess would never be allowed to do these.

So what was that royal nanny saying? She needed to think of something for addressing the query of the queen. She glanced down in contemplation, and saw her socks. Perhaps that was the solution. She eventually said, "If we could find the happiest child in the country, you could stand in that child's shoes, or even walk in her footsteps, and realize what it's like to be happy." Immediately, the princess insisted that the king send off a whole battalion of his guard to search out the happiest child in the country. "If you've found him or her," the princess said, "show me the children's shoes right away." Scanned and scanned the king's guard. The princess became irritated as the hours were days, and the days turned into weeks. He asked several times a day, "Did they find their happiest child yet? Where are the shoes that you told me? "The princess was worried about the waiting. Which would the happiest child's shoes look like?

Will they be trendy jeans, work shoes or brand-name sneakers? Which color would it be? Pink, red, yellow, blue? Happy shoes must definitely have been colored. Will it decorate them with roses, bows or bells? Will they have blinking lights like those she'd seen on television selling shoes? She just couldn't resist.

Yeah, day in and day out, the princess kept telling her royal nanny, "When are they going to bring me the shoes?" The day eventually came. The royal nanny came rushing into the princess' chamber with the news, "Your Highness, I've got some good news and some bad news," the little princess excitedly screamed, "Give me the good news first." "Well," the royal nanny said, "I am proud to say that we find the happiest kid in the entire country." "Where are my shoes then?" The princess asked, impatiently.

"This is the bad news," the royal nanny answered. "In the kingdom the happiest boy had no socks."

Chapter 5: Hypnosis Bedtime stories for kids

The dreaming and imagination is an important part of the action. A changed state of consciousness is normal, relaxed, and simple to attain for most children. Children like to discover their environments, and feel them. They want to communicate with others and the world around them. We are endlessly curious about the how and why of things, individuals, circumstances and themselves and have an appetite for dominance and mastery. This is from their inner realm of fantasy that infinite possibilities are available to them. A child may use imagination to alter or escape an uncomfortable situation, meet desires that are not fulfilled, recall the past, or imagine the future. The children want joy, safety, warmth and success. A child can develop maladaptive behaviour, either consciously or unconsciously, when physical, emotional, or environmental factors intervene. Hypnotherapy can be a very useful resource for a clinician who is interested in making the child achieve happiness, security and safety in a collaborative relationship. The hypnotherapeutic research stimulates and reinforces the innate interests of the infant for discovery, social interaction, imagination and innovation.

Children seek to explore life to the fullest degree possible; thus, it is not only enticing but successful to develop an imagination of a child with hypnosis. The effectiveness of a hypnotherapeutic treatment strategy depends on many variables which the acronym AH CREAM may recall. The most significant of these is the relation. The effectiveness of the infant-clinician medical relationship is crucial. The child wants to feel comfortable and the specialist optimistic. An accurate assessment, including a detailed history, of the issue is needed. The clinician must not only be knowledgeable and optimistic, but also credentialed, that he or she can help the child. A health care professional should not use hypnosis to cure a disorder without hypnosis which she is not qualified to treat. The child has to expect the hypnotherapy to succeed and to participate actively in the process. Hypnosis is not something that a child does; it is something that the child does for himself or herself, or allows it to happen when he has set the target that he wants to achieve. Another important variable in the effectiveness of hypnotherapeutic therapy is the willingness of the children to improve.

AH CREAM

A: Accurate assessment

H: History

C: Confidence, competence, and credentials

R: Rapport

E: Expectation

A: Active participation

M: Motivation

5.1. Pediatric Hypnosis and metaphorical approaches

If a picture is worth a thousand words than a million worth of a metaphor. Including parables, myths, and fairy stories, metaphors use abstract words to express a concept in an indirect way. Hypnosis is a valid psychological phenomenon, and a representation of the right brain. Metaphor may well be right brain expression. Metaphors have been used as a means of instruction in history. The Bible's parables, the Grimm brothers' fairy stories, and Aesop's fables are all popular with Western cultures. We learned the lessons of "The Little Machine That Could" and "The Hare and the Tortoise" as youngsters. These stories have much more effect than the "don't give up" mental admonitions and "long and steady race wins" ever could. Metaphors enable the hypnotherapist to interact with both the conscious and the unconscious minds simultaneously. The aware mind absorbs the words, the narrative, and the thoughts while by inference and connotation the motivational meaning is slipping into the unconscious. The unconscious mind examines the metaphor's broader meaning and personalized importance. The greater sense of the metaphor is rarely completely clarified in hypnosis, because the unconscious mind is left to wander far beyond the reach of reason. This pursuit of personalized relevance is what gives its potency to the metaphor. The motivation of the story is never clarified when a hypnotherapist uses metaphors, as it is in the fables of Aesop, allowing the protagonist to work out the meaning by himself — a far more effective experience. A metaphor's effectiveness is generated by a proper brain interaction that connects feeling, symbolic expression, and experience of life. The metaphor's purpose is to extend human consciousness. Since Vogel and Bogen developed a divided brain by transecting the corpus collosum * surgically, researchers discovered a great deal about how knowledge on the two brain hemispheres works. Though knowledge is shared cooperatively by the hemispheres, each has its own specific style or specialty. Logically and practically, the left brain operates to interpret the linear writing of the written word while the right brain actively processes the text in a systemic, tacit, and creative manner. To create the imagery and derive the essence of a plot, right-brain function is necessary. Clearly metaphor is the vocabulary of the right brain. The right hemisphere is triggered when conversation becomes metaphorical, since this is the hemisphere which is most involved in the interpretation of emotional and tactile experiences. Psychosomatic signs are mediated by primarily correct brain functions; psychosomatic disease may be a word in the right brain language.

Since the interpretation of metaphors is a valid brain condition, the use of metaphors in hypnosis may be a way of consciously interacting with the right brain in its own words. Because of the right hemispheric interpretation in both symptomatology and metaphorical context, metaphorical approaches to treatment can be even less time-consuming Metaphors enable the hypnotherapist to talk to the unconscious mind in abstract fashion. In a good context, the usage of symbols in the hypnosis results shifts. The audience cannot find the behavioral advice apparent. The idea may be so cleverly woven and ingrained in the narrative that the infant is unwittingly conditioned to improve without being admonished to do so consciously. This will add to a feeling of pride and a stronger sense of self-confidence. The child can be introduced to new possibilities, new viewpoints and different ideologies that metaphors. Metaphors can circumvent resistance, since they are perceived subjectively. The child sees the issue as one that happens to someone else; thus, she doesn't feel affected directly. Bringing constructive feedback to the unconscious is only one metaphoric goal. Metaphors bring the soul in. They also indulge in and strengthen confidence as they are non-threatening, allowing children to extend their minds, expand their horizons and grow knowledge. Metaphors tend to modify behavior patterns by changing the normal way of thinking of the victim. Restating the dilemma of the kid in a non-threatening metaphor allows the parent a clear viewpoint on the situation. Reframing lets the infant take back ownership of the problem to fix it. Throughout reframing, the details of a circumstance or occurrence remain the same, but modify the way the circumstance is interpreted or conceptualized, thereby changing the entire context. Sometimes, the infant has to use senses or experiences that are distinct from those he will usually use to achieve progress. With metaphorical approaches the unconscious mind of the infant is motivated to learn new ways of addressing weaknesses.

5.2. Marlene Worry Warthog – Hypnosis story for kids

Marlene was a Pig from Africa. She wasn't sweet, cuddly, or friendly, but she was beautiful. For several months Marlene was able to survive in an environment without any water. She liked taking sand baths, and loved rubbing her bristly body against trees and mounds of termites. Marlene was an extremely fast rider, even backwards. She couldn't see too well, but she would run back into a cave if she saw or sensed an intruder, and shielded herself with her very long tusks. When she was an infant Marlene came to sleep in the Ashland Zoo. She was called a "warthog" for having four big, lumpy warts on her nose. Harry nicknamed her the Hypnopotamus "Worry Warthog," since Marlene was concerned about everything. As she woke up in the morning, all Marlene's fears awoke with her: What if the sun is not shining? What if ashland zoo tourists think I'm ugly? What if the elephant Elkins gets sunburned and becomes rosy? All this imagination made the all-time warthog sound anxious.

Harry found Marlene was so concerned with what-if and thinking at times that she had stopped to have fun and to be comfortable. One day, he asked her, "I used to think over a lot of stuff, you know." "Which stuff?" Marlene asked.

"Ah, the things," Harry said. "I was thinking about all sorts of issues. For eg, I was really stressed when I learned that the zoo was going to move me to a new home." "You don't look worried now, "the worried warthog told me." It's how I've learned to use hypnosis," said Harry. "Hypnosis? What is it? "Marlene asked." This is a means of supporting yourself with your creativity," answered the hypno-potamus.

Marlene was snoring. "I've used my imagination before. I can tell no one likes me. I imagine it could rain on a picnic in the zoo and spoil everything. I imagine a rock landing on my foot and squashing it ... "Harry said," It's like taking an elevator with your imagination. It can take you down to a place you really don't want to be, a place full of worries and doubts, but it can take you up to incredible heights and beautiful places too. You should ride the elevator up to the clouds with your imagination, and fly like the eagles." "You do have a wonderful imagination, "Harry said." You can imagine all these negative things, but why not use the imagination to visualize good ones. You could use your imagination to help with sleeping. "The concerned warthog was worrying about what Harry had said to her. She said, "You know, Harry, sometimes friends are like elevators: they can encourage you and lift you up, or they can push you down." The concerned warthog agreed to use hypnosis and her imagination to strengthen herself after Harry and Marlene talked some more. She decided to push the elevator upwards, not backwards, to be the sort of buddy who raises up your spirits, not one who pushes you down. Marlene was able to take her imagination's elevator up to a marvelous spot. She pulled all her luggage full of fears and what-ifs with her when she climbed into the elevator. All that weight made the elevator so heavy it started to descend, not climb. Marlene had known she needed something to do. She used her dream to envision a WIFT, a What-if Garbage. She wanted the WIFT to be pink, as her dream color was white. She decorated it with daisies, because flowers she cherished. She made the WIFT from steel, because she needed it to be secure and sturdy. WIFT for Marlene looks a little like a mailbox. It had a slot for things to put in so you couldn't pull it back out. Marlene has been bringing all her fears and what-ifs into WIFT. She learned after a while that, if she began getting some anxious feelings ... ZING! They shot in on the WIFT right. That was Marlene's genuinely incredible WIFT, because it never got too loaded to bring things in, but it never let the stuff out again. It kept it secure until the time had passed for what-if, and then ... POOF! ... It WIFTED, and it only vanished mysteriously. After that, Marlene could remember to forget what-if she had put in the WIFT, or forget to remember when. And with the what-ifs in the WIFT before they did WIFT and POOFED, Marlene feels able to enjoy doing fun things. She could take her imagination's elevator up, up, up, up, and down.

5.3. Harry the hypno-potamus – A hypnosis story

Harry is a hippo. He resides in Zoo Ashland. Harry's got a great creativity. Harry's most favorite spot next to his house is a big mud puddle. There, he likes to run and pretend to be a submarine. Harry seems invisible to all the tourists who come to the zoo when he is all covered up in dirt. Dr. Dan is the doctor who looks after all the animals. He came to give Harry a shot of immunization one day, so that he would not get ill. Harry was scared, because he did not like needles. "I think you've got a wonderful imagination," Dr Dan said. "I'm going to teach you how to use your creativity, so that the shot won't trouble you." "Could you just be teaching me?" He was wondering. "Of course," Dr. Dan said. "Close your eyes, and pretend you're in your favorite place." "I am in a puddle of water," he said happily. "Next," Dr. Dan said, "imagine lying in the rain. No one will see you anyway. You're safe and sound. "Harry thought he was coated in mud all over him. The wet, moist mud felt good to his hands. He was feeling very relaxed. "Take a deep breath now," Dr. Dan said. "Imagine making bubbles in the water." Harry giggled, then breathed deeply. He feigned he was blowing bubbles. He had so much fun dreaming about his mud puddle that when the needle hit him, he had barely registered the slight touch. Harry was suffering a very bad toothache one day. Dr. Dan was going to see him. "Remember when I came to give you the immunization injection, how did your great creativity help?" But my tooth really does hurt," Harry said. Dr. Dan sympathetically smiled. "It will help her to hurt less in the imagination," he said. Harry breathed in heavily. "I'm set." "Close your eyes and pretend that you're having a lot of fun," Dr. Dan said. Harry screamed. "When I was a hippo," he said, "my daddy was telling me tales of Africa. There are big mud puddles, and lots of hippos will get together in the rain. "Harry closed his eyes and thought he was in a giant puddle of mud in Africa. There were plenty of hippos with him splashing and making bubbles in the water. He was so distracted worrying about the puddle of mud that he almost forgot about his toothache. One day, as Harry was playing in the puddle of his water, his friend Pam Penguin waddled up to him, flapping her wings in wonder.

"We're on a run!" She screamed. "The zoo is in the process of creating a new and safer environment for all of us to stay." "Harry feels his stomach ill. He needed it all to stay the same. He liked his very own mud puddle, the cozy, comfortable spot he had. Harry did not think he needed a new home. He felt embarrassed. Then Harry remembered how he had been taught by Dr. Dan to use his imagination to control his emotions and feelings. "I'm calling it hypnosis," Dr. Dan said. "It is about knowing something you did not think you learned. Helping yourself is dreaming.' Harry wondered what his new home would be like. Hippos can't see too well, but they smell amazing. Harry dreamed how his new house would look. He pictured the softness and coolness of his new mud puddle. The puddle of mud made him feel safe and comfortable, just as did the old one. Pretending to think about his new home helped Harry on moving day not to feel so scared. When Harry was taken to his new home by the zoo bus, Dr. Dan was there to welcome him. "You are so proud of me!" He was asking Harry. "When you use hypnosis to help yourself, I brought you a new sign I made for your new home. "HARRY, THE HYPNO-POTAMUS" said the message.

5.4. Molly Macaw – A hypnosis bedtime story

Molly was a rainforest macaw in Peru, from the Amazon. A macaw is kind of a parrot — actually, the parrot family's biggest and most stunning member. Molly's feathers were rainbow colors: violet, black, purple, orange and yellow. She was taken to the U.S. Ashland Zoo so everyone could see her stunning rainbow feathers. Everything was kind to Molly in the United States and she loved the zoo, but she missed Peru's tropical forest with its tall trees and beautiful flowers and she missed her friends. Molly had a lot of good friends living near the big Amazon River, with her. Frogs, monkeys, sloths, butterflies, snakes, and lizards were all present. A Toucan was her best friend. He had a big, colorful beak great for ripping open fruit for feeding. One day she was picking out one of her feathers when Molly felt homesick. It had seemed to make her feel better. She took out 2 more the next day. Soon, she learned to be so good at pulling off her feathers that even when she didn't feel bad, she did. It became a habit to take out her feathers, which she did so naturally she sometimes did not even know she was doing it. There were other things Molly did so well that she didn't even have to worry about it — for starters, sailing. That had been a good habit. Molly liked going to her dream spot — a tiny lake in the middle of the Ashland Park. She glanced down one day when she was standing on a tree there, and saw her reflection in the mud. "Two dumbbells! "The macaw screamed. "What happened to my lovely feathers? "The rainbow feather blanket of Molly was ripped and ragged. Most red feathers — her precious ones — had gone out. Molly was really upset. She dipped her beak under her wing to soothe her fears, and took out a thick, blue feather. "Oh, no!" "She kept squawking." I didn't say that I did. I have to stop, but I don't know how. "A friendly voice said," I can help! Molly looked down from her tree branch and, from the middle of the lake, saw Harry the Hypno-potamus swimming towards her. When he hit the beach, Harry said to Molly, "I wasn't listening deliberately, but you've got a pretty loud voice, so I couldn't help hearing what you're doing." Molly was so shocked that she didn't know what to do. "Dr. Dan, the zoo's veterinarian, taught me how I can control things I never thought I could use my imagination, "Harry said." Dr. Dan calls it 'hypnosis.' I am very good at it. That's why the sign over my new home says, 'Harry the Hypno-potamus.'" "I could definitely use some assistance," Molly stated. "If I don't quit drawing my feathers out I'll be as bald as an egg of a duck. Do you think that I should learn through hypnosis? "Yeah," Harry said. "Hypnosis is a lot like deliberate daydreaming. It's a way of thought that makes you come to your rescue. You should continue right now. "Molly sat back and made herself cozy on her tree branch. "Imagine the rainforest jumping away," Harry said. "Notice all the shades of color ... Listen to the sounds of the place — the birds, the monkeys, the insects, so familiar, so safe, so comfortable ... Feel the warmth of the sun and the gentle coolness of the breeze on your feathers ... Breathe in the place's smell, so relaxing, so peaceful ... Maybe you're going to taste your favorite rainforest food." "I should teach Shurcan how to intentionally imagine daydream," Molly said. "Shurcan is a brush but not a true toucan. I imagined him to fly across the rainforest, much as I do. Yet he is my companion and he came to keep me company all the way from the rainforest." "I think Shurcan will help you keep your feathers," Harry said." Every time you feel the urge to take a feather out, see and feel the large, beautiful beak of Shurcan Toucan pulling your bill away from your feathers. Molly kept her eyes closed, and thought. "Sometimes," Harry said, "when you get the need to take a feather you can imagine seeing a giant switch, like the sort that switches on and off a lamp.

You may use the click to turn off the temptation of dragging a feather. You could see a giant stop sign in your mind at certain moments where you felt like tearing your feathers.' Molly did all the stuff Harry said. Then Harry said, "Look into your imagination's mirror and see yourself as you'd like to appear, smell, and be, with all your beautiful, vibrant feathers." "It's easy," Molly said. Each day, she stared into the mirror of her mind and her fantasy feathers started to get prettier and more vibrant. One day, when Molly soared around the lake to her beloved tree, she glanced down from her branch and saw her reflection. "My feathers are thick and lovely too," said Molly. "I see how long my feathers in my tail have grown!" Whenever Molly used hypnosis to support cope with her problem, she felt very positive and proud of what she could do. She understood what she never did and managed what she never thought she could possibly do. She thought to support herself, deliberately hoping about the day. The next time she saw him she told Harry all of this. Harry showed her the wide smile of a hippo. "That's hypnosis," said happily Harry. "I find it the Power of Imagination," said Molly Macaw.

Chapter 6: Bedtime fairy tales for kids

An instance of a folk genre that takes the shape of a short story is a fairy tale, fairytale, wonder tale, magic tale, or Märchen. Usually, these tales involve creatures such as dwarfs, dragons, angels, fairies, giants, gnomes, goblins, griffins, mermaids, singing birds, trolls, unicorns or witches and generally spells or enchantments.

6.1. The Emperor's new clothes

There was a ruler many years back, who liked new clothing so much, that he wasted all his time dressing up. In the least, he didn't bother himself for his men; neither he want to go to either the theater or the hunt, save for the chances he was then given to show off his new clothing. The Monarch had a new suit for every other hour or two of the day; just as for any other monarch or queen, one is used to hearing, "He is having a seat in cabinet, "it was always like him, "The Queen is having a seat in his closet." Years gone by happily in the great city that became his capital; visitors appeared at the court every day. Once, 2 scoundrels were there in the court, introducing themselves as craftsmen. They gave away that they have the gut to weave beautiful design the most exquisite colorful items and intricate designs, from which the clothes created would have this characteristic of getting the person invisible to anyone that was not fit for the job and office he kept, or which was exceedingly plain in character.

"It truly must be stunning clothing! "The Emperor thought. "If I had this kind of dress, I could figure out at once what people are not suitable for their jobs in my domains, and even discern between the wise and the stupid! This material needs to be spun for me right away. "And he forced the two weavers to earn huge amounts of money so that they could continue their job un-interruptedly. Thus the two supposed craftsmen started 2 looms & worked quite busily, while they did little at all in fact. They demanded one of the expensive and rare silk and the genuine thread of gold; placed them in their own haversack; and then resumed their supposed crafting on the hollow looms till it started to get dark. "I'd like to see how craftsmen are going with my new dress weaving," the Emperor said to own self later spending some moments; however, he was very humiliated when he recalled that an ordinary man, and person not fit for his job, would not be able to witness the fabrication. He felt, of course, that there is no need for him to get worried about himself; but he would like to send someone else to offer him information about the and their work until he became disturbed in the matter.

All the citizens of the city had learned that the cloth was to possess the wonderful property; and they were all eager to know that how sharp, or how, unlearned their neighbors could be. "I will be sending my very old Cabinet minister to the craftsmen," the Emperor eventually said taking some moments, "he will better understand about the fabric; because he is an intelligent person, and he was the most suitable choice for the office then all." Finally the minister went to witness the craftsmen or weavers in the place where they were working with all their force, in the looms which were empty. "What could the significance be? "The minister said, widely opening his eyes' can't find the smallest piece thread on looms." But he didn't share his feelings openly. The impostors asked the minister quite politely to be so great to come nearer to their hand-looms; & after that they inquired him if he was satisfied with the arrangement, and if colors were perfect or not; while referring to the barren looms. The old minister searched and tried, for a very good cause, but he was unable to see thread on looms, nothing was present there. "So, then! "He wondered repeatedly. "I am a simpleton isn't it right? I never thought about myself that way; even if I am a simpleton, nobody will know it now. Is it true, that if I was not fit for my Job? Sorry, not to say that much. I'm never going to admit that I couldn't see the things. "Said one of the claiming to still function."You don't know if you like the stuff." "Yeah, it's fantastic! "The old minister replied, staring through his eyes at the loom. "These colors & the pattern, and the colors, yeah, I'll let know the king immediately how lovely I think they are." "We'll be very grateful to you," the cons replied, & then they called the various colors and explained the patterns of the supposed things. The poor minister heard keenly to what they are saying, because he had to tell the story again to the king & then the weavers begged for more gold & silk, stating that in order to complete the work they would need more of it. However, they packed all they were given into their kit-bags; & they proceeded to work at their hollow looms concentrating with evident zeal as before. So the Emperor sent another court officer to look how the craftsmen going on, & to see if the cloth might be ready soon. For this gentleman it was exactly the same as with the statesman, he inspected the working on both sides yet was unable to see anything except the hollow frames. "We think you did not liked the working as the minister did when he visited here? "The cons of the 2nd ambassador of the Emperor asked; at that moment, they made the same motions as earlier they did, and they spoke about the patterns and colors not there. "Of course I'm not dumb! "And the messenger thought. "It should be, I ain't ready for my fine, productive office! That's very odd; indeed, nobody's going to talk of it . "And then he admired the things he couldn't see and said he was so pleased by colors and shapes. "Off course, O our Lord," he said to his emperor as he came back, "the fabric prepared by the weavers is exceedingly marvelous." The entire city was buzzing about the glorious fabric that the Emperor had commissioned on his own expenditure to be woven. And so, when it was being manufactured in the loom, the Emperor himself wanted to see the expensive fraud. He had company of small number of court officials, The minister and the other member of court were also with the monarch who already had appreciated the working on project he went to visit the cons who, started much more efficiently as they were informed that the king is soon visiting them to see their hard work, even though they did not move the machine and a single thread. "Isn't the job absolutely superb?"The crown's two officers said, already reported. "If only your Majesty would be able to look at it! What a wonderful concept! What amazing color

! They started pointing and directing at the empty looms so that piece of art could be witnessed by others. "Who is that?" The Emperor said to itself. "I couldn't see it! It is a awful thing really!He started thinking if he was simpleton or incompetent to be a king? It will be the most imaginable thing — Oh! The fabric is lovely, "he said, loudly. "This attracted my absolute support." And he grinned most wonderfully, & gazed deeply on the hollow machines; for he did not suggest that he is unable to notice of what his 2 officers of his court had so much admired. His entire retinue labored their eyes now, wishing to find anything present on the machines, thus they were seeing the same the others were able to see; yet they all exclaimed, "Ooh, what a wonderful masterpiece!"then he suggested to use this splendid and mind-blowing stuff for upcoming meeting . "Splendid! Made of beauty!

Fantastic! "Both sides resounded; and both were uncommonly homosexual. The Emperor expressed in content; and rewarded the cons with the riband of knighthood order to be carried in their buttonholes, and the title of "Great Craftsmen." The criminals sat all night until the moment the ceremony was going to occur, & burned seventeen torches, thus, everybody could see how impatient craftsmen are to finish the Emperor dress. They tried to take off fabric from the webs; they cutter the air by their sharp knives; yet they started sew with help of needles while having no yarn. "Oh! "At last, they screamed. "The new robes of the Emperor are set! "Then the king arrived inforn of the weavers with all the great men of his court; and the imposters brought up their hands, as if by keeping up something, stating, 'these are the pants of your Majesty! Here's the fire! Here's the manteau! The whole suit is so comfortable and light in weight anyone may imagine that, when wrapped in it, this, indeed, is the great quality of this wonderful thread. "But this was real that nobody was being able to see anything, beautiful make, all the courtiers said. If the Lord majesty happily remove the dress you are wearing, we want you to try the new dress we made, " Thus the kind removed his dress, and the imposters tried to posed to fit the King in his wonderful new dress; the King moved round, side by side, before the glass-looking. "How beautiful my Lord is looking, & how precisely they are match in his new garments! "Everyone screamed. "What a makeover! What sorts of shades! These are royal garments too! "The canopy to be carried in the Court over your Majesty is pending," the head of the ceremony stated. "I'm very happy," the Emperor replied. "My new dress match right?"He asked to turn side and round again in front of the glass that shines, so that he could appear to inspect his lovely suit. The bedchamber lords, anybody to bear the train of his Majesty, looked like they were raising the bottom of mantle on the ground; and refused to carry anything; for they must not reveal something like ease or not fitting for their Jobs.

And now the King marched down the streets of his capital shaded by the canopy, in the middle of the procession; & every citizens found nearby, and many at the door, screamed, "Ah! So magnificent are the latest robes of our King! What a splendid ride to the mantle there; and how graciously the scarf falls! "In brief, no one should encourage him to wear such much-admired clothes; for he would have proclaimed himself not fit for job or a simpleton. Of course, not any of the different suits of the Emperor has ever made such an impact as these unseen individuals. "Rather the King has absolutely none on it! A small kid said. "Earn the voice of truth!" His father exclaimed; and whispered from one to the other the point he kid has made. "But he has absolutely nothing on!" All the people have finally yelled aloud. The King was vexed, because he realized the citizens were right; so now he felt the procession would have to proceed! And the bedchamber lords suffered more suffering than ever before, trying to tie up a bus, though in fact there was no bus to catch.

6.2. The Pig man

Once upon a time there was a poor Prince, who had a kingdom. His empire was very small, but still large enough to get married; so he decided to get married. To the Emperor's daughter it was definitely very sweet of him to say, "Will you have me? "But he did so; for his name was known far and wide; and a hundred princesses replied," Yes! "And" thank you so much. "We'll see what this princess has written. Hear!

It happened that where the father of the Prince laid buried, a rose tree grew up — a most lovely rose tree that blossomed once in every five years, and even then bore just one bloom, but it was a rose! It smelled so good, that he who inhaled his scent forgot all worries and sorrows. Moreover, the Prince had a nightingale, who could sing in such a way that it appeared as though all the sweet songs were living in her little throat. So the Princess was to have the rose and the nightingale; and accordingly they were set in large silver caskets, and sent to her. The ruler had them carried into a large hall where the Princess played with the court ladies at "Visiting;" and when she saw the caskets with the presents, she clapped her hands with joy. "Ah, if only a little pussy-cat! "She said, but the rose tree came to view with its lovely rose. "Wow, how beautiful it is!" All the ladies of the court said. "It's more than pretty," the Emperor said, "it's really cute! "Yet it was kissed by the Queen, and almost able to weep. "Fie, Baby!" She said. "It's totally not made, it's normal!" Before we get into a poor mood, let's see what's in the other casket," the Emperor said. So the nightingale came out and sang so delightfully that no one could say something ill-humored about her at all. "Fantastic!" Charming! "The ladies screamed, as they all chatted with French, each worse than his friend.

"How much the bird reminds me of the musical box belonging to our blessed Empress," an old knight asked me. "Oh heck! The same voices, the same execution." "Yes! Hey! Yea! "The Emperor said, and wept in remembrance like a child." I'm still hoping this isn't a real bird," the Princess said. "Yes, it's a real bird," the ones who brought it said. "Well then let the bird go," the princess said; and she declined to see the prince in a meaningful way. He was not to be discouraged, however; he daubed his face over black and brown; pulled his hat over his head, and knocked at the entrance.

"Good day to the Emperor my Lord!" He said. "Will I get a job at the Palace?" Why, yes," the Emperor replied. "I want someone to look after the goats, because we have a lot of

And the Prince was named "Imperial Pig man." He had a filthy little room next to the pigsty, and he was sitting there all day and working. He had made a fairly little kitchen-pot by the evening.

Small bells hung all around it; and when the kettle boiled, these bells tinkled in the most charming way, playing the old song, "Ach! Dear Augustine, Everything's gone, gone, gone! "Yeah!" * * Honorable Augustine!

The whole thing is gone, gone, gone! "But what was even more interesting, whoever stuck his finger in the kitchen pot's smoke, instantly smelled all the dishes that cooked on every stove in the city — this was something very different from the rose, you know.

Now it happened that the Princess marched that way; and when she heard the tune, she stood still and seemed pleased, for she could play "Lieber Augustine;" it was the only piece she knew; and she played it with one finger. "Why is this my piece," the Princess said. "Fair enough, the pig man must have been well trained! Go in and ask him for the instrument's size. "Then one of the court-ladies would run in, but first she drew on wooden slippers. "What are you going to take for the kitchen-pot? "The lady said.

"I'll get ten Princess kisses," the pig man said.

"Hell, hell! "The lady said.

"I can't exchange anything for less," the pig man rejoined.

"He's a brutal fellow! "And the princess replied, and went on; but when she had gone a little way, the twinkling of the bells was so lovely." Dear Augustine, Everything's gone, gone, gone! "Keep tight," the princess said. "Tell him if he's going to get ten kisses from my court girls." "Sorry, sorry! "The pig man said. "Die Princess's ten kisses, or I keep myself the kitchen-pot." "Neither will it be! "The Princess said. "But all of you stand before me so that no one can see us." And the court-daughters stood before her and spread out their clothes — the pig man had ten kisses, and the princess — the kitchen pot. That was adorable! The pot boiled the entire evening, and the whole day after.

They knew perfectly well what had been cooking throughout the city at every fire, from the chamberlain's to the cobbler's; the court-ladies danced and clapped hands.

"We know who's got chili, and who's got dinner rolls, who's got cutlets, and who's got bacon. How inspiring! "Yes, but keep my secret, for I am the daughter of an Emperor."

The Prince's pig man — that is, the Prince, since no one realized he was anything than an unfortunate pig man, could not let a day pass without operating on anything; he eventually designed a rattle that, when it was swung round, played all the waltzes and jig tunes that have ever been heard since the world was created.

"Oh, that's fantastic! "As she walked by, the Princess said. "I have never seen any more pretty compositions! Go in and ask him for the instrument's price; but he won't have kisses anymore! "He'll get a hundred Princess kisses! "The lady who was to inquire said.

"I don't think he is right with his senses! "The Princess said, and went ahead, then she paused again, after she had gone a little way. "Art must be promoted," she said, "I am the daughter of the Emperor. Say him that he should have ten kisses from me, like he did yesterday, and will take the others from the court ladies." "Oh-but we shouldn't like that at all! "They said. "What are you talking about? "Princess asked.

"If I should touch him, you should certainly. Know you owe me something.' And the ladies had to go back to him. "A hundred Princess kisses," he said, "or else let everyone have their own! "Hold on ring! "She said; and as the kissing went on, all the ladies gathered behind her. "What might be the explanation for the pigsty near to such a crowd? "The Emperor, who came to the balcony just then, said, wiped his lips, and put on his spectacles. "They are trial ladies; I ought to go down and see what they're all like! "Then, at the bottom, he picked up his slippers because he had slipped on them.

He walked very quickly until he reached the court yard, & the women were so enthralled numbering the kisses that they should all go on equally, that they could not consider the King. The emperor sprang up on his toes. "What's it all? "Once he realized that actually what is happening, he said, and with his slipper he turned the Princess's mouth, took the eighty-sixth kiss. "Watch out! "The Emperor said, because he was excessively angry; and the princess and the pig man were driven out of town. The Princess was now crying and shaking, the pig man scolding as the rain pouring down. "Woe to me! I am unhappy man! "The Princess said. "Like I have just dated the beautiful Prince! Oh! How unlucky I am!" And hence the pig man marched next to a bush, cleaned off his skin the black and brown pigment, took off his filthy garments and stepped out in his princely vestments; he appeared so majestic that the goddess also couldn't resist kowtowing to him I have come to scorn you," he stated. "You wouldn't have an noble Prince! You couldn't reward the flower as well as the merlin, but you were happy to kiss the swineherd for trumpery games. You're done properly." Instead he went right back in his own tiny realm and closed the house door in her face. Now she would say, everything is gone, gone, gone!"

6.3. The real princess

Once upon a time there was a Prince hoping to marry a Princess; but then she must be a true Princess. In hopes of meeting such a woman, he traveled across the world; but there was still something wrong.

Princesses he noticed in abundance; but it was difficult for him to determine if they were true princesses, for now one thing, now another, about the ladies seemed to him not quite right. He eventually returned much cast down to his palace because he wished too badly for his wife to have a true princess. A terrible tempest emerged one evening, it thundered and lightened, and in torrents the rain poured down from the sky: it was as black as the ground. A loud banging at the door was heard all at once and the old King, the father of the Duke, went out himself to open it. It had been a Princess standing outside the house. She was in a sad condition with the rain and the wind; the water trickled down from her hair, and her clothes clung to her body. She claimed she was a true Queen. "Oh, my goodness! We'll see that soon! "The old Queen-mother thought; but she didn't say a thing about what she was going to do; instead she went softly into the bedroom, stripped off all the bed-clothes, and put three little peas on the pillow. She then laid twenty mattresses over the three peas and overlaid the mattresses with twenty feather beds. The Princess was to spend the night on this bunk.

She was asked the following morning if she had fallen asleep. "Wow, very poor indeed! "She replied. "I've barely closed my eyes for the entire night. I don't know what was in my room, but there was something heavy beneath me, and I'm black and bruised all over. It has done me so much good! "Then it became clear that the lady must be a true queen, because through the twenty mattresses and twenty feather beds she had been able to feel the three little peas. Anything but a real Princess may have had such a fragile feeling? The Prince made her his wife accordingly; now he's sure he'd find a true Princess. Nevertheless, the three peas were put in the mystery cabinet, where they are now to be found, until they are misplaced. Wasn't this genuinely delicate lady?

6.4. A most Different Voyage

Through personal experience, any Copenhagen resident understands how well the doorway to Roddick's Clinic feels; but because it is likely that those who are not Ottawa residents can also review this little piece, we must give a quick overview of that at all.

The comprehensive tower is isolated from the sidewalk by a very high fence, so far away were the heavy metal walls, in all honesty, it has been said, some really slim fellows had once pushed itself into a night to go out and make his small checks to the area. Most challenging area of body to handle on these instances was, obviously, the head; there, like it is the instance in history, fast-headed men get across better. So much for the intro, then.

One of its young people, whom head may be seen like the densest in a sense of physical just, had the watches that evening. It started the rain and burst into streams; yet, in view of such two barriers, the young person was forced to be out, if only for a couple of minutes; and to inform the doorkeeper that, he felt, was very pointless, if he might escape via the railings with an arm. Inside, the galoshes, that the warden had overlooked, lie down; he seldom imagined for a moments that they had been Great deal of money's; and they gave him good customer care in the cold; so he placed all. The problem now was that he could push itself via the grating, just as he had never yet done it. Well, He was standing here now.

"I'd gotten my head open to Paradise!" he stated unwillingly; then immediately passed over it, quickly and painlessly, because this was quite large and heavy. But maybe they had to get across the remaining physical body!

"Ah! I'm too stout," he grumbled loud, repaired as if in a voice figured the brain was the worst aspect of the question-oh! Oh! I can't even push myself in!" He tried to take back his under-hasty hands, but he just couldn't. There was space enough even for his heart but that's it. His first impression was of rage; his second was that his patience had sunk to null. He had been got in very hard and terrible condition by the Fortune Shoes; and, alas, it has never happened with him to desire itself home. In even heavier streams the wicket-black clouds spilled off their innards; no man had to be found in the road. To meet the bell is what he would not want; he had no use in screaming out for help; however, how embarrassed he would have been found trapped in a pit, like an outsmarted fox! How does he pull itself around! He knew plainly that being an inmate before midnight, or although even late throughout the dawn, was his irreversible fate; otherwise the smith had to be removed from reality to put away the stalls; thus all this wouldn't be achieved so easily as he might conceive regarding it. The entire Charity Academy, on the other side, is in action; all the fresh stalls, without their not so courtier-as hot of seafarers, could pursue those because of interest, and it would welcome him with such a wild "hoorah!" as he was sitting in his public square: there is a crowd, a growling, or reveling, and heckling, 10 fold less out of the lines about Jewish people several years before-" O, my blood is piling up to it.

Yet you don't have to accept the relationship is now over; it's getting too worst.

Night gone, as well as the next day; still no one came to get the Socks.

At the King Street small theatre, "Tragic Readings" had been provided in the night. The building was packed with suffocation; and a new poetry by Wells was amongst other parts to recite. C. Anders, entitled, My Aunt's goggles; the details were almost as follows: "The certain individual having an aunt, which spoke with special talent in card-telling, but who was continually assaulted by people that wish to get a glimpse in to the futures. Nevertheless, she remained full of magic regarding her craft, in which a specific set of magical glasses were doing her invaluable service. The hospital's young person, who seems to have overlooked his aventure of the previous night, has been among the crowd. He has on the footwear; for whatever legal holder has yet existed to assert them; so he felt they are just the answer for him, plus it was just so very dusty outside.

With much humility he lauded the beginnings of the verse: he also considered the concept unique & successful. And that the conclusion of it, as the Rhine is very negligible, showed the author's lack of imagination in his opinion; he was beyond extra ordinary, etc. This was a perfect chance to have done something insightful.

In the meantime, he was fascinated because of the idea, he must like to own that kind of duo of goggles for himself; otherwise, just by wearing them circumspectly, he could be able so that can see into the minds of men, which, he felt, would be much more fascinating than just seeing what will occur in coming year; for that we would all know at the right time, but never the other." can now," he said to himself, "fancy the entire row of ladies and gentlemen seated on the first row there; if one can only look into their hearts, yes that might be a revelation, kind of bazar. I would consider for particularly a big milliner's shop in that lady yonder, so oddly dressed; the shop is bare, but it wants to clean surface all along. But among them, there would be some fine, stately shops too. Ah, Sorry! "He sighed," he said, "I am aware of the fact that which one of everything is beautiful; but there's still a tittative young shopkeeper who's the one thing in the shop that's wrong. All will be wonderfully placed out, & we would say, 'Come in, gentlemen, come inside, this is where you can find anything you really want.' Oh! I wish I might go in to Heaven and take a ride straight into the cores which are here! "& look, you see! That was the signal to the boots of Fortune; the every man was shrunk & a very peculiar voyage from the hands of the spectators' front row began now. The very first spirit where he passed was that of a center-aged woman, yet he immediately saw himself in the space of the "Organization for the Healing of the Twisted and Disfigured," whereby sculptures of malformed legs are shown on the gable in bare truth.. And there was one distinction, the deposits were collected at the patient's arrival in the institution; though they were confined in the heart & protected since the voice people went along. We were, including casts of non-male mates whose most carefully maintained physical or cognitive dysfunctions are here. He glided into another female heart with the writhing of an idea; although it looked like a huge, holy fane to him. The white innocent dove flickered on the altar. How gladly he would have sunk on his feet; though he need to go to the adjacent soul; although he was hearing the echoes of the organs, and he was feeling like he has become much more stronger and healthier; he thought it was not appropriate to move in the adjacent place that was revealed by a poor haymow with a ill bed-ridden mother. Yet the bright sun of God shone from the window which was open; beautiful flowers bowed on the roof from the boxes which are made of wood, and 2 birds which are sky blue in color sung rejoicing, as the ill mother implored her devout daughter for God's greatest blessings. He now crawled into a butcher's shop on feets & hands; there was nothing but meat on either leg, both upside down. It was the core of a most sophisticated wealthy man, who is sure to find his name in the database. Now, he was in this good gentleman's wife's head. This was an ancient, dilapidated, mouldering twig. The portrait of the husband was treated like a wind vane, associated with the doors in some manner or another, and then they closed & open themselves as the stern old husband turned round.

There upon he stumbled into a sleeping accommodation made up completely of glass, just as at Rosenberg Castle; yet the lenses are exacerbated astonishingly. On the ground, in the center of the room, the person's trivial "self" stood, like just a Dalai-Lama, very surprised in his own superiority. He instead dreamed that he had reached a syringe-case full of spiky bolts of all sizes. "This is an old maid's head, sure," he said. He still did not understood it was the soul of a soldier. It was the heart of a young soldier; a man with talent and emotion, as people have said. Now he came out from the last soul in a row in the greatest perplexity; he was finding it difficult to properly gather his thoughts, and fancied that his very vivid manifestation came along with him. "Well done heavens!" He sighed. "Surely I have a turn of mind to lunacy — it's terribly warm here; and Blood in my arteries is hot, so the brain is smoking as fire. "But now he recalled the evening before, when his brain had been jammed between the hospital's iron railings. "No way! Is this how it is," he said. "I will do it in time: a shower could be best for me under these circumstances. I wish I'd still be on the upper side. In these Russian (vapor) pools, the individual stretches to the side or form, and as he gets used to the sun, he goes up to the roof, where the vapor is, of course, warmest. In this way he slowly ascends to the top. And so he lay in the vapor-bath on the top bank; still in his boots and galoshes with whole garments over him, however the hot droplets comes down burning from the top onto his nose.

"HI!" "He screamed and climbed down. Through him, the bathing attendant vociferated a big shout of astonishment as he beheld a man clad in the water. However, the other one maintained enough existence of sense to communicate to him, "'this is a call & I earned it! "Although the 1st thing he wanted as soon as he gets back would be to put a big tumescence on his rib cage and take his insanity away. He was suffering from chest pain and blood extravasation back the next morning; and besides the horror, which all he had learned from Fortune's Shoes.

In the meantime, he became fascinated by the notion-he will like to own a set of glasses himself; otherwise, maybe by wearing them assertively, he will be allowed to look into the minds of the people, that, he felt, would be even more fascinating than seeing what will occur the year after; for it we would all learn at the right moment, but not the other.

I may still, he said to itself, decor the entire section of sir or madam seated at the front of the line; if one would only see in the souls-yes, it would be a revelation-a kind of souk. Within this lady thar, so oddly clothed, I will have to find for sure a big milliner's shop; in this one that store is bare, just she needs to wash it well plenty. That was the signal to the Boots of Fortune; the entire person diminished along and a very peculiar trip across the cores of the spectators' first line started now. The very first heart through which he passed is that of a woman of the middle ages, yet he soon liked itself in the space of the "Establishment for the remedy of the bent and disfigured," whereby sculptures of deformed legs are shown on the wall in bare nature. So there was a distinction, the casting are obtained at the patient's arrival in the organization; but now they were held in the core and protected as the sound engineers went along. They are, including sets of women friends who quite diligently maintained physical or mental deformations are here.

He slid into a woman heart with both the wasp-like writhing of an idea; yet this seems to him as a huge, sacred fane. The white innocent dove flapped over the crucifix. How happily he should have fallen on his toes; yet he must go to the new soul; but he always noticed the peeling sounds of the heart, but he indeed just seemed to be a younger and stronger man; he felt ashamed to step in the adjacent temple that was unveiled by a weak garret with such a sick bed-ridden mother. Yet the bright sun of God shone via the air vent; lovely flowers bowed from either the wood bloom-boxes on the wall, or two moon-blue birds joyfully sang, as the ill mother urged her holy daughter with the greatest grace of God almighty.

He then crawled into a butchers shop with hands and feet; there was nothing but meat at only on either leg, both above and below. This was the core of a far more decent wealthy man, who is sure to find his name in the Database.

Suddenly, he was in this respectable chap's wife's core. This was an old, decrepit, rotting twig. The image of the husband is used as a climate-cock, associated with the windows in some manner or another, and then they raised and shut themselves as the strict old husband turned around.

Hereupon he stumbled into a bedroom entirely composed of reflections, like the one at Rosenberg Fortress; but here the lenses enhanced to an extraordinary extent. On the ground, in the center of the room, the individual's trivial "self" stood, like just a Dalai-Lama, very surprised at his own superiority. He instead dreamed that he had reached a needle-case full of pointy needles of all sizes.

"It's an aged maid's head, sure," he said. Still he was wrong. This was the spirit of a young soldier; a man with talent and passion, as people stated.

He then emerged of the last core in the line in the highest bewilderment; he was also unable to place his head clear, and liked that his too wild imagination had flee with him.

He grinned: "Dear lord!" "Surely I possess a tendency of insanity - 'this is incredibly warm here; my adrenaline is boiling in my bloodstream and my brain is smoking like a flame.' And then he recalled the significant incident of the night before, how his brain had been stuck among the hospital's iron railings. "No way this is how it is," he added. "I ought to do it in time: in these conditions a Russian bath will do me well. I just wished I'd really be on the higher bank. So he laid in the mist bath on the higher bank; still with both his garments on, with his shoes and rain boots, as the warm drops scalded from either the roof on his chest.

"Hoolloa!" he yelled and leaped. On its side, the bathing assistant emitted a loud scream of amazement as he glimpsed a person clad in the water.

The other one however, maintained a decent frame of thought to say to him, "'This was a bet, and I earned it!' But the only move he accomplished as soon as he went back was to place a big rash onto his chest and take his insanity back out.

He used to have a swollen chest as well as a bruised spine a next afternoon; and except the scare, it was all he had learned from Fate's Boots.

6.5. The Fir tree

A good little Fir Tree stands out in the park. The position he had was a really nice one: the sun shone on him: there was plenty of that as for fresh air, and a lot of big-sized comrades, pines as well as firs grew around him. Yet the little Fir deserved to be a grown-up tree too badly.

He didn't worry of the warm sun and the fresh air; he didn't care for the little cottage kids who played about in the woods in search of wild-strawberries and prattled. The kids always came along with a whole pitcher full of berries, or a long line of them threaded on a stick, and sat down by the young man, saying, "Ah, how beautiful he is! What a cute little tree! "But the Tree couldn't stand to hear this.

He had shot up a good deal at the end of a year and after another year he was another long bit taller; for with fir trees you can still tell how many years they are from the shoots.

"Yeah, yeah! Were I just a tree as big as the others,' he sighed. "I would then be able to stretch my roots, and look into the big world from the tops! The birds would then create nests among my branches: and when there was a wind, I was able to bend with as much stability as the others! "Neither the sun-beams, nor the birds, nor the red clouds that flew over him morning and evening, brought any joy to the little Boy.

As the snow fell on the ground glittering in winter, a hare will always hop along and leap straight over the little Tree. Yeah, that made him so irritable! But there were two winters past, and the Tree was so big in the third that the hare was compelled to go around it. "Growing and rising, growing older and becoming tall," the Tree thought—"that is the most wonderful thing in the world after all! "The wood-cutters also came in the fall and felled some of the largest branches. This happened every year; and the young Fir Tree, which had now risen to a rather comely height, trembled at the sight; for with noise and cracking the majestic huge trees dropped to the ground, the limbs were lopped off, and the trees appeared tall and bare; they could hardly be recognised; and then they were loaded in carts, and the horses pulled them out of the forest.

Where were they headed? What was it that made them?

When the swallows and storks came in Spring, the Tree told them, "Don't you know where they were taken? You didn't get to see them anywhere? "The swallows knew nothing about it; but the Stork looked musing, shook his head, and said, 'Yes; I believe I know; I encountered many ships as I flew here from Egypt; there were splendid masts on the ships, and I went on to say that they smelled too much of fir. Can I applaud you, for most majestically they raised themselves up on top! "Yeah, I was as old as I could float around the sea! Yet in fact how does the sea look? And what is it? "It will take a long time to describe that," the Stork replied, and he walked off with those words.

"Rejoice in growing up! "The Sunbeams said. "Rejoice in your vigorous growth, and in the fresh life which moves within you! "And the Wind kissed the Fir, and the Dew wept over him with tears; but the Fir did not understand.

As Christmas arrived, very small trees were cut down: trees that were were not quite as large or of the same age as this Fir Tree, that could never rest, but would still be down. Such young trees kept their leaves, and they were still the best looking; they were put on carts, and the horses pulled them out of the jungle.

"Where do they want to go? "The Fir asked. "They aren't taller than I; there was one that was much shorter; so why did they keep any of their branches? How are they being brought in? "We know that! We do know! "Sparrows chirped. "We opened the windows in the city below! We wonder they're taking where! They are awaited by the greatest splendor and the greatest magnificence one might imagine. We looked through the windows and saw them in the middle of the warm house, adorned with the most beautiful stuff, gold apples, gingerbread, toys and several hundred lights! "What, what? "The Fir Tree pleaded, shaking at each bough. "What now? Then what happens? "We haven't seen anything else: it was absolutely amazing." "I'd love to ask if I'd be meant for such a wonderful future," the Tree screamed with happiness. "It is easier yet than jumping the water! Such a loneliness I am waiting for! Is Christmas going yet! I'm tall now and my roots are growing like the others that were taken away last year! Ah, ah! I was on the cart yet still! Were I with all the splendor and magnificence in that warm bed! Yes; so something greater, something bigger, will certainly follow, or else will they ornament me in this way? Even still, something larger still needs to follow — but what? Yeah, how long I have, how much I have to endure! I don't even know what the matter is with me! ""Rejoice with us!" "Wind and Sunlight said. "Rejoice in a new generation of your own! "But the Tree was not at all happy; it rose and rose, was green both in winter and in summer.

People who saw him said, "What a beautiful tree! "And He was one of the first to be chopped down after Christmas. The ax cut deep into the pith; the Tree fell with a sigh to the earth; he felt a pang — that was like a swoon; he couldn't think about joy, but he was sad to be removed from his family, from the spot where he had risen up. He knew well that no longer could he see his poor old friends, the little bushes and flowers surrounding him; maybe not even the birds!

The exit was not satisfying at all. Just when he was dumped in a court yard with the other trees did the Tree come to himself and heard a man say, "This one is perfect! We don't want the rest. "So two servants arrived with a rich livery and carried the Fir Tree to a large and elegant drawing room. Portraits were displayed on the walls, and two large Chinese vases with lions appeared on the coverings by the white porcelain stove.

There were also big easy-chairs, silk sofas, big tables full of photo-books and toys worth hundreds and hundreds of crowns — at least the kids said so. And the Fir Tree was trapped upright in a cask packed with sand; but no one could see that it was a cask, for all around it was draped green fabric, and it sat on a big gaily-colored carpet. Ah, ah! How the Tree rumbled! What would have happened? It was painted by the cooks, and the young women. Small nets cut out of colored paper hung on one branch, and each net was filled with sugarplums; and golden apples and walnuts were hanging among the other boughs, looking as if they had grown up there, and little blue and white tapers were placed between the leaves. Dolls that searched the entire universe like men — the Tree never had seen it before — were seen among the leaves, and a large star of gold tinsel was set at the very top. It was very sumptuous — beyond superb description.

"What a night! "None of them said. "Oh that'll shine tonight! "Ah, god! "The Tree figured. "If the night was not here! If only the tapers lightened! Even then, I wonder what's going to happen! Maybe the other forest trees will come over and look at me! Maybe the sparrows will smash the window-panes! I wonder if I'm going to take root here, and stand lined with ornaments in winter and summer! "He knew a lot about this — but he was so restless that he got a pain in his back for sheer desperation, and that with trees is the same as a headache with humans.

Now the candles were lighting up — what brightness! What magnificence! In every bough the Tree trembled such that one of the tapers set fire to the foliage. It famously blazed out.

"Let's help! Help!Help! "Old ladies screamed, and they put out the fire easily.

The Tree didn't even dare to tremble now. What a mess it stood in! He was so nervous that he would loose some of his splendor that in the middle of light and sunlight he was very bewildered; when unexpectedly both folding doors opened and a group of kids jumped in as if they were disturbing the Forest. The older people silently followed; the little ones remained very still. But it was just for a moment; then they screamed that they re-echoed the entire place with their rejoicing; they jumped around the House, and took off one gift after the other.

"By what do they mean? "The Tree figured. "Whatever happens now! "And the lights burnt down to the very roots, and they were taken out one after the other when they burnt out, and so the children had permission to loot the Forest. So with such brutality they crashed upon it that all the limbs cracked; if it hadn't been tightly rooted in the ground, it would surely have tumbled down.

The kids played around with their pretty playthings; no one looked at the Tree except the old lady, who peeped between the branches; but it was just to see if a fig or an apple left had been overlooked.

"What a novel! A story to tell! "The kids were moaning, drawing a little fat guy to the tree. He stood under it and said, "We're in the shade now, and the Tree will listen too. But I'll tell you only one story. Now what are you going to have; that was Ivedy-Avedy, or Humpy-Dumpy, who tumbled downstairs, and still returned to the throne and married the princess after all? "Ivedy-Avedy," others screamed; "Humpy-Dumpy," some screamed. There was such a crying and bawling — the Fir Tree was quiet alone, and he said to himself, "Shall I not bawl like the rest? Am I to do anything? "For he was a corporation, and he had done what he was meant to do.

And the man spoke of Humpy-Dumpy who tumbled down, who nevertheless rose to the throne, and eventually married the queen. And the kids clapped their hands, and wept. "Oh, just keep driving!

Do go ahead! "They wanted to know about Ivedy-Avedy too, but just about Humpy-Dumpy the little man told them. The Fir Tree remained very still and lost in thought; the wooded birds had never mentioned the like of that. "Humpy-Dumpy dropped downstairs and still the princess married him! Ja, hey! That's the way the universe is! "The Fir Tree felt, and believed everything, because the man who told the story looked so amazing. "Ok, fine! Who knows, maybe I, too, could fall downstairs and get a princess as a mom! "So he looked forward to the morning with excitement, as he wanted to be filled with decorations, playthings, vegetables, so tinsel again.

"I'm not going to be shivering tomorrow! "The Fir Tree thinking. "I'll love all my splendor to the max! I will hear Humpy-Dumpy's tale again tomorrow, and maybe Ivedy-Avedy's tale too. "And the Tree remained still and in deep contemplation throughout the night.

The servant and the housemaid arrived in the morning.

"Now the splendor will start over again," the Fir thought. But they pulled him out of the house, and climbed the stairs into the loft: there they left him in a dark corner where no daylight could reach. "What did you mean by this? "The Tree figured. "What am I going to do? What am I meant to hear now I wonder? "Then he rested in reverie against the wall lost. He never had ample time for his reflections; for days and nights passed by, and no one showed up; so when anyone actually did, it was only to bring those nice trunks out of the way in a corner. The Tree remained much unseen there; it looked as if he had been totally overlooked.

"'This is natural season now! "The Tree figured. "The ground is rough and heavy with snow; men can't plant me now, so I was put in shelter here before spring! How considerate it is! After all, how kind man she is! If it wasn't always so cold here, and so dreadfully lonely! Not a hare, though! And it was so nice out in the field, when the snow was on the ground and the hare sprung by; yes — even when he leapt over me; but then I didn't like it! It is really terribly lonely here! "Squeak out! Squeak out! "A little mouse said, peeping out of his hole at the same moment. And then came another little one. They snuffed and rustled among the trees around the Fir Tree.

"It's dreadfully cold," the mouse said. "But for that, it would be delightful here, old Fir, wouldn't it? " "I am by no means old," said the Fir Tree. "Most of them are considerably older than I am." "Where are you from," the Mice asked; "and what do you do? " They were so extremely curious. "Tell us about the most beautiful spot on the earth. You've never been in there? Were you never in the larder, where cheeses lie on the shelves, and hams hang from above; where one dances about on tallow candles: that place where one enters lean, and comes out again fat and portly? " "I know no such place," said the Tree. "But I know the wood, where the sun shines and where the little birds sing." And then he told all about his youth; and the little Mice had never heard the like before; and they listened and said, "Well, to be sure! How much you have seen! How happy you must have been! "

"And I! "The Fir Tree said, thinking about what he wanted to do for himself. "Yeah, in fact those were fun days." And then, as he was decked out with cookies and candles, he told of Christmas-eve. "Oh," said the little Mice, "how blessed you are, old Fir Tree! "I am not ancient by any stretch," he said. "This winter I've come from the woods; I'm in my prime, and I'm only pretty small for my generation." "What wonderful stories you say," the Mice said: and the next night they came with four other little Mice to hear what the Tree said: the more he told, the better he recalled himself; and it seemed as though those days were very good. "So they could still come — they might still come! Humpy-Dumpy has dropped off, and he has a bride! "And at the moment of a lovely little Birch Tree rising in the park, he thought: to the Fir, it will be a charming queen.

"Who are the Humpy-Dumpty's? "The Mice asked. So then the Fir Tree told the whole fairy tale, for he could recall the single word thereof; and the little Mice leapt up to the very top of the Tree with joy. Two more Mice came the next night, and two Rats again on Sunday; but they said the stories weren't fascinating, which vexed the little Mice; and they, too, began to think of them not as funny. "Knew you just one story? "The Rats asked. "Just that one," the Tree answered. "On my best evening I read it; but I didn't realize how pleased I was then." "It's a dumb tale! You don't know one of candles with bacon and tallow? Can't you remember any tales about bigger ones? "No" the Tree replied.

"Alright then," the Rats said; and they went off. The little Mice even stayed away at last; and the Tree sighed: "After all, as the sleek little Mice sat around me and listened to what I told them, it was very fun. That, too, is over now. So when I'm taken out again I will take good time to enjoy myself. "But what was it to be? Why, a quantity of people came in one morning and went to work in the loft. The trunks were pushed, the tree was ripped out and put down on the floor — rather rough, it is true — but a man dragged him up to the steps, where the sun was shining. "We'll launch a happy life again now," the Tree thought. He felt the first sunbeam, the fresh air — and now he was out in the courtyard. Everything moved so hard, there was so much going on around him, the Tree forgot to look at himself. The court adjoined a garden and it was in flowers; the roses hanging over the balustrade so young and odorous, the lindens were in bloom, the Swallows flew by and shouted, "Quirre-vit! My husband has just arrived! "But they didn't want a Fir Tree."I'm going to truly love life now," he said exultingly, spreading out his branches; then, alas, they've all been dried up and gray! He lay in a field, between weeds and nettles. The tinsel's golden star was always on top of the tree, sparkling in the sunlight. Two of the merry kids were playing in the court yard who had danced around the Fir Tree at Christmas and were so delighted at his sight. One of the youngest ran and ransacked the golden star. "Now look what the disgusting old Christmas tree actually holds! "Trampling on the trees, he said, so that all of them broke beneath his foot. And the Tree beheld all the beauty of the roses, and the freshness of the garden; he beheld himself, and wished he had stayed in the loft in his dark corner; he thought of his first youth in the forest, of the merry Christmas-eve, and of the little Mice who had listened to Humpty-Dumpty's tale with such enjoyment. "'Tis over-it's not yet! "The poor tree said. "Had I ever been glad I had cause to do so! Yet 'tis past now,' tis past now! "And the boy of the gardener cut the tree into small pieces; a whole heap was lying there. Behind the big brewing copper the wood flamed splendidly and it sighed so deeply! Every single sigh was like a weapon. The boys played in court, and the youngest wore the gold star that the Tree had on the best night of his life on his breast. It was done now, though — the Tree's gone, the plot finished. All, all was over — any tale would eventually finish.

6.6. The Snow Queen

First story

There was once a evil sprite there, but he was the most mischievous of all sprites. One day he was in a very good mood, for he had made a mirror with the ability to make everything that was nice and lovely to look bad and evil when reflected in it; but that which was nice for nothing and seemed hideous was magnified and enhanced in ugliness. The most stunning scenery looked like boiling lettuce in this mirror, and the strongest men were terrified or seemed to stand on their heads; their features became so blurred that they could not be recognized; and if someone had a mole, you could be sure that it would be magnified and scattered over both the nose and the ears.

"This is fantastic pleasure! "The sprite said. If a positive idea went through the head of a man, then the mirror showed a smile, and the sprite grinned heartily at his clever discovery. All the little sprites who went to his school — for he had a sprite school — told each other that a miracle had happened; and that it would only be fair to see how the future truly looked like now, as they figured. They raced about with the mirror; and at last there was not a blurred land or human in the mirror that was not reflected. Then they thought they'd go up to heaven, and make a laugh there. The higher the mirror went, the more sadly it grinned: they could hardly keep it steady. They went higher and higher again, more and more to the stars, until suddenly the mirror shook with smiles so horribly that it shot out of their hands and dropped to the ground, where it was broken in a hundred million bits and more. And now it acted even more evil than before; for some of these bits were scarcely as big as a grain of sand, and they spread about in the wide world, and as they came across the heads of the men, they remained there; and then they were something perverted, or they had just an eye for that which was bad. It was because the very smallest bit had the same strength the whole mirror had. These people have got a splinter in their neck, and it caused a shudder, as their neck was like a block of stone. Many of the shattered bits were so large they were used for windowpanes that one could not see one's friends though. Some bits were set in spectacles; and it was a sad affair as people put on their glasses to see properly and well. Then the evil sprite grinned until he nearly screamed, because his imagination was tickled by all of this. The delicate splinters were already floating in the air: so now we're going to know what's next.

Second story

A little boy and a little girl

In a big area, where there are so many houses and so many inhabitants, that there is no roof left for anyone to have a little garden; and where, on this basis, most people are compelled to be content with flowers in pots; there lived two little ones, who had a garden that was a little larger than a flower pot. They were not brother and sister; but as if they were, they cared for one another. Their parents lived the reverse. They occupied two garrisons; and where one house's roof crossed that of the other, and the gutter extended down the extreme end of it, there was a narrow doorway to each house: one just had to jump over the gutter to get from one doorway to the other.

There were big wooden boxes in which the children's parents planted vegetables for the garden, and little rosetrees besides: in each box there was a rose, and they grew splendidly. Now they thought about placing the boxes across the gutter so they almost reached from one window to the other, and looked like two walls of flowers. The peas' tendrils hung over the boxes; and the rose trees shot up long branches, twined around the windows, and then twisted one to another: it was almost like a triumphant arch of foliage and flowers. The boxes were very high, and the kids knew they shouldn't be creeping over them; so they often got permission to get to each other out of the windows and sit among the roses on their little stools, where they could play with delight. This joy had come to an end in winter. Perhaps the windows were frozen over; but then they heated copper farthings on the burner, and put the hot farthings on the window frame, and then they had a capital peep-hole, very beautifully rounded; and a soft, polite eye was peeping out of each — it was the little boy and the little girl looking out. His name was Kay, Gerda his hers.

They could get to each other in the summer in one jump; but in the winter they were forced to go down the long stairs first, and then up the long stairs again: and there was quite a snowstorm outside.

"The white bees are swarming," Kay's old grandmother said.

"Do white bees choose a queen? "The little boy asked; for he understood that there was always one of the honeybees.

"Yes," the grandmother said, "she flies in the thickest clouds, where the swarm lives. She's the biggest of them all; and she can never keep silent on earth, but heads off into the dark clouds again.

She flies over the streets of the city many a winter night, and peeps in at the windows; and then they froze in such a beautiful way that they appear like roses." "Yeah, I saw it, "both the kids said; and then they realized it was real.

"Will the Snow Queen come inside? "The little girl said.

"Let her just walk in! "The little boy said. "I should have put her on the fire then, and she would have melted." And then his grandmother patted his head and told him other stories.

Little Kay was at home in the evening, half undressed, crawling up the window on the chair and peeping out of the little door. A few snow-flakes had fallen, and one, the biggest of them all, remained lying on the bottom of a flower pot. The snowflake became bigger and bigger; until at last it was like a young girl, wrapped in the finest white gauze, consisting of a million little star-shaped flakes. She was so exquisite and fragile, yet of ice, of bright, shining ice; and she lived; her eyes stared fixedly, like two stars; yet in them there was neither peace nor rest. She nodded to the window, and winked at her hand. The little boy was terrified and leapt out of the chair; it looked to him that a huge bird soared by the window at the same time. There was a harsh frost the next day — and then the spring came; the sun shone, the green leaves emerged, the swallows constructed their nests, the windows were opened, and the little kids sat in their lovely garden again, high up on the leads at the top of the property.

The roses flowered in unparalleled elegance that year. The little girl had heard a hymn in which there was something about roses; and so she thought about her own flowers; and she sung the verse to the little boy, who then sang it with her: "The rose in the valley blossomed so beautiful, and angels went down there to meet the children."

And the kids held each other by the side, kissed the flowers, gazed up at the bright sky, and talked as if they were really seeing angels. What perfect summer-days! How lovely it is to be out in the open, next to the fresh rose-bushes, who look like they will never finish blooming!

Kay and Gerda stared at the picture book full of beasts and birds; and it was then — the clock in the tower of the church was just struck five times — that Kay exclaimed, "Ah! I experience such a strong heart pain; and now something's getting in my eye! "The little girl was holding her arms around her waist. He checked his eyes; little was to be done now.

"I know it's out now," he said; but it wasn't. It was just one of those bits of glass that had gotten into his eye from the magic mirror; and poor Kay got another one right in his face. Soon, it will feel like frost. It didn't hurt much but it was there.

"Do you weep over what? "He asked. "You feel very hideous! There's nothing for me on this issue. Ah, "he said in a moment," the rose is cankered! Oh look, the one is pretty crooked! These roses are really ugly, after all! They are exactly like the box in which they are rooted! "And then with his foot he gave the box a quick kick and picked up all the roses.

"What is it you are doing? "The little girl cried; and when he saw her terror, he picked up another rose, stepped through the room, and rushed away from the beloved little Gerda.

He then wondered when she took her picture-book, "What horrid beasts do you have there? "And if his grandma wanted to tell them stories, he would always interrupt her; besides, if he could afford it, he would stand behind her, put on her spectacles and mimic her manner of speaking; he would copy all her habits, and then everyone would laugh at him. Eventually, he was able to mimic everyone's gait and manner on the street. Anything that was odd and irritating about them — that Kay learned how to imitate: and all the people said at these moments, "The boy is actually very clever! "But it was the glass that he had in his eye; the glass that sticked in his heart that made him taunt even little Gerda, whose whole soul was devoted to him.

His games were very different now from what they used to be, they were so quite experienced.

When the snowflakes were swirling around one winter's day, he stretched his blue coat's skirts and captured the snow as it came.

"See this glass clear, Gerda," he said. And every flake seemed bigger and appeared as a glorious tree, or a stunning star; look at it was splendid!

"Look how wise! "And Kay said. "This is much more fun than real flowers! They are as reliable as possible; there is no flaw with them, except they have exploded! "It wasn't long after when, when one day Kay came with big gloves on, and his little sledge on his back, bawling straight into Gerda's ears," I've got permission to go out to the square where the others are playing; "and he was off in a moment.

Some of the boys in the marketplace used to tie their sledges to the carts when they went by, and then they were pulled along and had a nice run. It was so very money! Just when they were at the very height of their pleasure, a big sledge went by: it was painted very white, and everybody in it was bundled up in a rough white fur cape, with a rough white fur cap on his head. The sledge rolled twice across the square, and Kay tied as hard as he could on his sledge, and he pulled away with it. On they went faster and faster onto the next street; and the person who was driving turned to Kay, and nodded to him in a polite way, as if they knew one another. The guy smiled at him every time he would untie his sledge, and then Kay sat quietly; and so on they went until they came beyond the town gates. Then the snow began to rain so thickly that the little boy couldn't see the length of an arm before him, but he continued on: then he abruptly let go of the rope he carried in his hand to get free from the sledge, but it was of little use; the little car he pushed on with the wind's speed. He then screamed as hard as he could, but no one heard him; the snow was falling and the sledge was going forward, and often it gave a jump as if they were driving through hedges and ditches. He was very afraid, and attempted to recite the Lord's Prayer; but what he could do, he could only recall the table of multiplication.

The snow-flakes grew bigger and larger, until they looked just like great white fowls at last. Suddenly on one side they flew; the huge sledge stopped and the guy who was driving fell. It was a lady; there was snow on her cloak and hat. She was tall, slim in figure, and of a gleaming whiteness. She was King of the Snow. "We've gone fast," she said; "but it's cold frozen. Come under my bearskin. "And she placed him next to her in the sledge, wrapped the fur around him, and he looked as if falling in a snow-wreath. "Did you still feel cold? "She asked, and she kissed his forehead. Oh! This was colder than ice; this reached his very core, which was still like a frozen lump; it felt to him as though he was going to die — but for a moment, it was very nice to him, so he didn't mind the cold surrounding him. "My dumbbell! Then don't miss my sled! "He thought about it for the first time. This was tied there to one of the white chickens, who flew behind the broad sledge along with it on his back. Kay was kissed once more by the Snow Queen, and then he remembered little Gerda, grandma, and everything that he had forgotten at home.

"You won't get any more kisses now," she said, "or else I'd have to kiss you to death! "Kay looked down upon her. She was very pretty; a better, or a more stunning woman he couldn't imagine himself; and she no longer emerged from ice as before when she stood outside the window and winked at him; she was fine in his mind, he didn't doubt her at all, and he told her that he could measure in his head and with percentages, even; that he knew the amount of square miles there was in the distance Then it seemed to him that what he learned wasn't enough, so he looked up in the vast open space above him, so flew with him on it; flew high above the black clouds, as the wind moaned and whispered as if singing an old melody. They soared over forests and fields, over oceans and other lands; and the icy wind swept swiftly underneath them, the wolves hurled, the snow crackled; over them soared huge crying crows, but the moon, very big and brilliant, shone higher; and it was on it that Kay gazed through the long winter night; while he slept at the foot of the Snow Queen by day.

Chapter 7: The Risky Ventures of Zorian – Adventurous bedtime story for kids

There once lived a widowed nobleman and his only child, a daughter called Zapata, in an ancient & crippling home by the delirious ocean shore. Given their high birth, living in poverty, so hapless that the plains & forests of their small realm had been auctioned one by one to purchase essential goods for surviving. He knew that Zapata will be lonely and a miserable condition practically as when he will pass away, he brought her up as not as a girl but as boy, she was not aware of riding the horse instead ride it as an expert so magnificently, outclass her dad in his one of the favorite fencing competition., and even swim like a mermaiden & the good disposition Zapata got it genetically from her mom. Zapata never felt odd or different while she was being brought up different other kids.

By the end of the evening of October, when the violent air stream from the ocean rocked their petty old home to its very base and set the tattered draperies on the walls, Zapata's dad passed away. He left behind a golden florin, a subunit of copper, & only crippling home. The sum of money was adequate for Zapata to spend almost a week or two, Zapata will be on her own when this little amount on money will be gone, what would she do? The father of girl had asked her to visit the King & request him for his guardianship; but the Castle or Palace of the Monarch was very far away from her home, and Zapata flinched from lending his hand in front of someone or the distant road.

The courageous girl eventually decided to pave her footings to survive in this world. She got all the guilder of gold and moved to a small town which was nearby, and purchased an attire. After that she went on to dress her hair up so should looked like a guy, dressed like a boy, wearing clothes she just bought she started moving towards the main bazar of the area to look for any position

At that time it was a usual practice that if a person is a looking for a job as domestic worker he may go near the fountain in that market and the people who were in need of a worker also went to get one there.

No one was present waiting on the owner's side of the spout as Zapata came into the bazar, but contrary to this, preparing for the 1st owner who would come, there was a small number of loud and brazen lairds and bellhops. Zapata, or Zorian, as she called herself now, strode proudly over & entered this party, pounding her heart fast with the excitement of the fantastic venture.

Then a knight-errant-errant, riding on a horse and luring the other cart by Baulk wobbled across the square's gravel stones, and moved towards the spout, shouting to the bellhops to come to him. However, despite the summons of the horseman, the bellhops ignored him and nobody was moved. Curious to learn the reason for this contempt, Zorian asked a nearby bellhop and she was enlightened that the knight-errant was nothing but Enchanter, and that no bellhop or laird should represent him the reason his palace was plagued by trolls, demons, and every kind of frightening spirits. Today, Zorian wasn't a funk, or beggar, as the quotation goes, can't be selector. And, much to the bellhops' amazement, Zorian went over to the Knight, who was apoplectic with tension & longing and told him that he is ready to work for him. The Knight-errant bade Zorian mount the horse that he held; and frisked in the background chatters of the hooting of the bellhops, lairds and masters.

They rode all day long, until the sun was about to set and Zorian found himself on the edge of an uncivilized, abandoned moor. In the ballistic trajectory of the sky, under the light sunlight, there has not been a leaf, not just a home, not even a shepherd's shack to been seen, but the huge desolate wasteland that rolls up and falls to the very edge of space. The sun sank lower and lower; cold grew, & a blue smoke fell. Came Sunset, a dark, green dusk.

Suddenly, Zorian beheld the magical dwelling from a moor hillock down. A huge submerged swamp confronted him, which was starting at the base of the mountain and going interlaced, until its parent side was lost in the darkness catching up. The air stream fussed the brushes at the top, and the fading sunset was gleaming still on the horizon broad bog had captured none of its shine, and lied Packed of turquoise-coiled fog, delicate quagmires, and obscure black islands. A hideous cry of weeping, out cried by some moor witch, echoed across the mist, freezing the gore in the veins of Zorian; so to a response of the shout, hundreds of will-o'-the-wisps emerged, darting and spinning. A great black rock up rose stood exactly in center of this awful marsh, the fortress was standing on this giant solid rock, its walls and battlements set against the blazing light of the moon. Ghostly lights flickered in the glass, now white, now dark. At the edge of the swamp, the Enchanter reigned his horse and wept until the prancing conjuror-fires rushed from both parts of the wet land to him. After a while a path was discovered leading through the marsh to the palace, an enchanting path that which was disappeared in the back of the horses like smoke disappears in the winter breeze. The ghost-fires followed the Enchanter to the first door of his castle; then, rising rapidly high up into the clouds, they fled in all sides like astonished fowls.

The doors opened up by themselves, mysterious and horrible beings left, and shiny, whirling fire globes fled through the courtyard of the castle hissing. As soon as they were entering the palace, the Knight-errand moved himself and starred on Zorian with his blazing pupils.

"Boy," he said, "let nothing you listen or watch scare you. Be told you can't be affected by any force or spirit. In the universe a single ghost is more powerful than me, who has more strength then me and that is terror itself. Be courageous, keep your heart's doors fixed and closed in front of this terror; be loyal, and you will never have reason to remorse for being here. "And Zorian, who was courageous by definition, felt bad of permitting the demon terror to strike at his heart's door, and vowed not to slip his valor ever, whatever could happen. And the lad held faithful to this determination throughout the passage of time he remained at the Enchanter's side. Firstly, for being confident, he needed to fight to overcome his distrust of any of the baggards; so the time tickled away and no demons or baggards again tried to bother him, he became habitual of their appearance & finished by giving no further heed to all than to the might dark clouds that flew croaking across the quagmire. The small bellhop was so obedient and brave that when a year was finished, the Enchanter asked him to stay another year again, offering him lavish bonuses if he lived. Nonetheless, after the 2nd year was finished, Zorian had a desire to witness the normal lands again, and convinced the Enchanter he needed to go.

"Alright," replied the master, who admired the courageous bellhop's bravery, you're a courageous and trustworthy lad. Here's a gold bag for your pay, and here's three presents to honor your bravery and goodwill. "He opened a barrel of copper and carried out a tiny glittery fowl with spread pinions hung from a fine glittery cord, a golden ring, and a ruby sphere decorated with a white band. "This small fowl," the Enchanter added, "will shield you against the curses of any magician or demon whose strength is not greater than my power, and would start singing when you go into secret dangerous situation; this passe-partout will unlock any gate throughout the might lands; and if you get distracted form your path, you just have to place this barrel on the table, and it will start rolling itself and safely take you home. Remember, if you're ever in dangerous trouble, contact me, and I'll come and rescue you. "And Zorian was obliged by the Enchanter and brought his presents back to the world. Yet he was so sweet and generous that he quickly gave away all the golden coins he had received to the poor, then he was forcefully sent to look for some other situation. He joined the emperor and his wife of the Twelve Towers service at long last.

This royal family, famed both for their kindness and goodness in Fairyland as well as for their riches & grandeur, but they only had a son, Prince Wezel. He was famous for his valor and bravery that no other warrior earned such fame. He busted the green cavern dragon out of the realm of his father; he was in combat with 3 evil witches side by side, and killed all of them; he had given an awful spell to the diamond palace that was imposed over it.

When Zorian joined the Monarch & Queen's service, these wonderful guardians were sent their son on a tour to his brother, the ruler of the plan, and Zorian was commanded to follow the nobles, warriors and troops their convivial company, who were set to make the voyage. Prince Wezel was advised to visit to his uncle's, in the hope that he might fall for the ward of his uncle, the lovely Princess Rosamond, according to the company's gossip.

So, however, it was many days the company was in travel on the road for a few days, Prince Wezel, who looked after as closely as a decent captain looks over his men, was conscious of Zorian's courage, trustworthiness and humble appearance, the small bellhop and asked him to be his private laird. Oh, Oops! He was no longer advanced than Zorian's little post, though outwardly remaining a post, was the running away girl Zapata at heart. Though she struggled against her own heart as much as she might, all in vain, as she realized that she had fallen in love with this beautiful prince Wezel. She nevertheless happened to sign or indication of her love to escape her the Wezel thought of her only a small bellhop, and if she was going to utter it may be to unearth the secret she had kept for a quite a period of time so effectively.

One day, as the caravan was passing by a lovely country, Zorian, so we still have to keep naming Zapata, followed closely behind his prince, Prince Wezel saw a beautiful ruby-red flower something like a ruby plant, glittering by the side of the lane. The exact instance, as if it were real, the little glittery fowl Zorian worn in his neck sang a few simple notes. "What a beautiful flora!" The Prince said. "I want to take it." And when Zorian spurred ahead of him, he almost came off the horse to collect the flower, Zorian came forward tossing magical flower to it into a trench. "Oh, how naughty you are bellhop!" all the knights and women screamed. The business was traveling a few kilometers on, when the Prince immediately got his eye on a stunning knife with jewels lying on the road. Exactly the same instance the little glittery fowl was singing a few simple alarm notes.

"What a knife! "The Prince shouted, I want this.' And he was about to uninstall & take the knife, when Zorian stepped in, grabbed the weapon, and hurled it into a ditch.

"Oh, what a non-sense thing! "Troops and women screamed.

The business was moving constantly for a couple miles further now, and the Prince again seen a lovely enchanted forest on the roadside. In the bushes, fowls of many shades sang, spouts were sparkling and played in the sunshine and the sweetest of music was being played. The glittery fowl sung harder and much louder exactly the same time.

"How stunning place is this! "Prince screamed. "Let's go inside and explore its beauty." So Zorian dashed to the Prince's side, imploring him not to enter, claiming the place was magical, and any danger may come upon him.

All the officers and their wives, maybe a little annoyed of a bellhop would know better than they did, chuckled at little Zorian, and even Wezel grinned at him, saying, "That's just fun, little Zorian," and squeezed through the gate of the garden. Nothing happened about a little while or so, & the first person who went in ridiculed the Zorian; until the whole company had reached the place, there came a scare sound of thunder, and all but the Wezel and Zorian, who were covered by the magic of the Enchanter, were transformed as rocks. The rumble of echoes had barley quit to roll when two terrifying demons with the heads of lions charged across that place toward them, grabbed the Wezel and took him along with them. Zorian lingered in the garden alone. Night was coming soon.

Now, a witch was the owner of the magical forest, who had a daughter so hideous that only the strong spells of her mother could not make her attractive. However, despite her ugliness, the daughter of the witch thought herself reasonably stunning, and she often imported her mother to invite the princes of the castle that she found deserving of her hand. So the old witch offered lovely dances and parties to which all of the neighborhood's worthy young kings and princes were invited, but as soon as the witch's daughter emerged on her hideous face with a horrid smirk, the young men were sure to make their excuses and ride away.

Lastly, the old witch, who had just had a severe reprimand from her daughter for not punishing the Prince of Hendriya after that Prince had refused to ask her for a dance, could no longer bear the scolding of her daughter and vowed to trap the first prince. The latter came past her yard, and compel him to embrace her hideous daughter, willy nilly. In her pit, poor Wezel had entered, and the witch had thrown him into a dark cellar, trying to turn him to her will by frightening him. The hideous daughter had suddenly looked through the prison's keyhole and, at first glance, fallen in love with Wezel.

The witch was only deciding what to do next when her lion-headed servants told her that one of the company had defied her spell and walked around the yard. So the witch put on her invisibility cloak, and going down to the garden, found poor Zorian wandering under the trees disconsolately. Instantly she witnessed tiny glittery fowl that had saved him from her magic. Being terrified of the beauty and still powerless to do any harm to the little boy while the fowl was in his hands, she resolved to rid herself of Zorian by taking her palace, gardens, and everything else around the globe. So, she muttered a spell, and everything was gone.

The next morning when Zorian woke up and found the castle was gone, his heart sunk. He did not despair, however, but took the little scarlet ball that his lord, the Enchanter, had given him out of his pocket, placed it on the table, and bade it lead him back to the Enchanted Forest.

At Zorian's own pace, the little ball suddenly started rolling ahead; at night, it glowed with a scarlet light. Next day, month after month, the scarlet ball went on; it led Zorian across hill and down dale, through the land of the people who had only one hand, through the area of the dwarfs, and through the valley of the singing trees, never halting until it reached the witch's garden entrance.

A year had gone by, meanwhile, and the witch had done everything she could to persuade Prince Wezel to embrace her hideous daughter during that year. She had attempted to frighten him first, then attempted to win him by offering him splendid fetes, then tried to intimidate him again, but because the Prince was not to be terrified or cajoled, she came to the end of her wits. She told the Prince that if he didn't agree to marry her daughter the very next day, she'd turn him into a hare and put her dogs on him. The Prince did not react to her awful warning, and the witch stepped on and planned for the greatest of marriages. Zorian arrived in the garden that evening.

As it was late, and the moon, a quarter full, had vanished behind a curtain of clouds, Zorian arrived unseen at the door of Wezel's prison, for the witch had locked him up so tightly that she hadn't taken the time to locate a guard. Oh, Sorry! The poor Prince laid at the top of a high tower, and twenty different doors stood between him and the ground, each unlocked by a different key.

Yet Zorian was not to be daunted, and taking the key that the Enchanter had given him from his bosom, he unlocked one door after another before he entered the Prince's inhabited cell.

The unfortunate Prince laid bound on a straw bed, struggling to read a book by single candlelight. He became despondent, as he had agreed not to marry the ugly witch maiden but to let himself be ripped in half. You would be sure he'd been delighted to see Zorian.

"Dear Zorian," the miserable Prince said, "if I had just obeyed your counsel, everything would have been fine." And he begged Zorian to tell him where he had been all year long. So Zorian described his exploits to the Prince.

Now the chains the Prince wore were cruelly riveting around him, and because there was no lock on them, there was no use in the magic ring. Nevertheless, Wezel tried to work them off at length; but in doing so, he hurt his foot and discovered to his dismay that he was still able to walk along. Gradually the warm air and the movement of leaves started to foretell the dawn's arrival. Eventually, just as the dawn-star has begun to fade, Wezel and Zorian rushed through the twenty doors from the jail and raced to the highway.

But when the wicked witch learned Wezel's flight, they had driven just a few miles, and, dreadfully enraged, ordered her dragon car to be ready so she could go after him. So the car rolled out, and the witch leaped into it and climbed into heaven. Hearing the dragons' hissing and screaming in the air, Zorian and Wezel attempted to hide under some trees; but the witch spotted them immediately and pronounced a spell to turn them into hares. Even while the witch's hate was swift, Zapata's woman's heart was faster, and she sacrificed herself for the man she loved, she flung the chain and the golden fowl over the head of the Prince. She had transformed a moment later into a little gray hare crouching at the foot of Wezel. At the same time, the wicked witch, who had entered her castle, let loose her pack of fearsome hunting dogs, who soon picked up the hare's trail and came in full cry running toward her. The unfortunate Prince picked up the hare and hobbled on as soon as he could, ignoring the awful agony it caused him, but the dogs raced a hundred times faster than he did. The pack came closer and closer, their red tongues clinging out of their black throats. Through a good chance, even when the pack leader was not more than fifty feet away, Zapata had enough intelligence to recall the vow given to her by the Enchanter and to call upon him. Immediately a solid glass wall rose from the ground behind Zapata and the Prince, as high as a castle tower, and the pack, hurrying on, found themselves pulled by their prey. Snarling and screaming, they hurled themselves against a pillar of magic; but in vain.

The Enchanter himself stood before them in another moment, and brushing the hair with his hand, returned Zapata to its human form. Nevertheless, she still wore Zorian's clothes, and the Prince always thought of her as a child.

Suddenly a shadow appeared behind them on the table, and everyone looked up and saw the evil witch and her hideous friend, riding out in the dragon car to celebrate the gruesome death of Wezel. The Enchanter caused the dragon car to vanish suddenly, and the witch and her daughter plunged into a pond tumbling through the air and became disgusting little fish. Then the Enchanter took Wezel and Zorian back to the castle of the witch, where the tables were set, and the meal was served to celebrate

Wezel's wedding and the daughter of the witch. Last, of all, he rescued the business of Wezel from the spell of the witch.

Now, one of the ladies, when she learned how the witch had attempted to pairWezelwith her aunt, and when she saw the wedding arrangements, told the Prince that it was a shame that Princess Rosamond was not at home so that after all there would be a wedding there.

"A wedding? No, "Wezel said," not until I met a wife who proved to be genuine and loyal as a little Zorian." "She's already here, "the Enchanter said. And Zorian touched his sword. There was a burst of flame suddenly, and out of it, Zorian no longer emerged, but herself, Zapata. Her hair had grown again long, and she was clad in the most magnificent gowns by the Enchanter. No lovelier girl was ever to be seen on earth. Maybe you're confident the Prince walked in, took her by the side, and claimed her for his bride. Shortly Wezel's mother, who had been invited by the Enchanter, came, and after all, there was a marriage. The Enchanter returned to his castle on the Black Rock when the merrymaking was over, while Wezel and Zapata returned to their own country, and lived there happily to a right old age.

Conclusion

Recall what it was like to have a parent or grandparent sit on your bedside at night as a young child and read a story that gave you permission to escape into your own fantasies? Why did the magic of the plot affect you, encourage you, turn you into a special but yet familiar character, and lead you through encounters you could not have experienced before? How did you learn something different about yourself in the process, sense the excitement of hitting the end of the tale and share a special connection with the teller? Stories, fables, and parables have been successful and favored methods from time immemorial for transmitting knowledge, teaching principles, and exchanging valuable life lessons. Just hear those four words, sometimes spoken, "Once upon a time. ." is like an immediate transition from fact to pretense, or to a modified processing point. We are like a hypnotic injection, an invitation to participate in a special interaction with both the teller and the characters of the plot. These are words which invite the listener on a journey into an imagined world where reality can be suspended and learning can be strong. These are an introduction to a different domain of interaction in which listeners become entranced, concentration is concentrated and one may feel the fictitious hero's emotions. We welcome participation in a relationship where teller and listener share an intimate connection. Stories exhibit many essential characteristics of efficient communication:

1. They're really social.

2. They teach with appeal.

3. They bypass opposition.

4. They engage with creativity, and cultivate it.

5. We gain expertise in problem-solving.

6. They build future result.

7. They call for rational decision-making.

We embody all of the qualities that we try to build in our relational interactions with children in this manner, and when we participate in the cycle of listening to stories, our interactions with ourselves, with others, and with the world as a whole will certainly change. Although we may or may not realize it, story-telling may create relationships, question concepts, offer templates for future action and promote comprehension. We can see some of ourselves in the characters and teller and be affected, little by little, by their behaviors, beliefs, and skills. It has been said before that we can never un-hear it once we have heard a story that everything might have changed forever. Stories are also a rational and efficient means of interacting with children in a constructive way. In this book all sorts of amazing bedtime stories have been compiled to help parents with their kids effective learning, sleep and evolution in to a confident person.

Lightning Source UK Ltd.
Milton Keynes UK
UKHW051350140121
377031UK00003BA/12